Jenny in Corona

Stuart Ross

Jenny in Corona

Stuart Ross

Tortoise Books
Chicago, IL

FIRST EDITION, SEPTEMBER, 2019

Published in the United States by Tortoise Books

www.tortoisebooks.com

ASIN: XXX
ISBN-10: 1-948954-06-0
ISBN-13: 978-1-948954-06-8

Cover image by Nicholas Sutton Bell
Cover artwork by Kim White

Tortoise Books Logo Copyright ©2019 by Tortoise Books. Original artwork by Rachele O'Hare.

Contents

SHAME IS SINCERITY LEAVING THE BODY   1

MAINSTREAM   33

THE FUTURE APRIL   63

MIDNIGHT GIRLS, AFTERNOON WOMEN   97

BOBBY D.   135

THE BLINDFOLD FAITH   177

Shame is Sincerity Leaving the Body

Why do you need roots when you have gravity?
— *Lee Lozano*

I have twelve years of experience. I have responsibilities. I believe in cops. I believe in the Constitution. April is the future and so are the stars. Live one day at a time and make it a masterpiece, because tomorrow will be here before you know it. Duke Ellington is white. I learn the word *genre* on MTV, the word *pearl* from a Prince song. Tape deck, record player, Lincoln Head Cent coin collection and *Golden Guide* volume about stars. I read the definition for *white dwarf* and that's how I feel. A stellar remnant composed of degenerate matter. Very dense.

Daddy tells me I'm getting taller. My father nurtures my gift for music, sending me to a special school on the Upper East Side. I receive an hour of private piano lessons with Mrs. Osorio, and an hour in a group class focused on rhythmic movement. These are the most exciting hours of my week. Mrs. Osorio is the most beautiful woman I know. She teaches me the word *goiter* for what's going on around her neck. I love the way she swings her parcels from the rich lady stores on Madison Avenue. She weighs the world in cashmere and karats. She doesn't dye her graying hair. I dream she dines alone on the West Side, in Chinese-Italian fusion restaurants that serve Hawaiian passion cocktails.

She sings "There Will Never Be Another You."

I can't bear to look.

She sings "I'll Remember April."

I must look. April is the month of my birth.

When I see Mrs. Osorio I see only her blouse. Everything a blouse, even her Christmas socks out of season.

She tells her students the truth. We nod and promise we know what she's talking about. She says, don't bother using Mozart to help you study, use him to help you make love. Don't bother using Beethoven for Sturm und Drang, she warns, use him to predict the future, as he himself did when he peeked the rhythms of ragtime in the Arietta of his final piano sonata. In 1826, Schubert had the most creative year in the history of mankind. Call him Louis Armstrong, not Louie, call them jazz compositions, not heads or tunes.

We sing "Day by Day" by Stephen Schwartz and fold our hands like penitents.

We sing "Two Little Flowers" by Charles Ives and I wish I was a little girl holding a flower, but not the little girl who dies, the little girl who must keep on living, to bear and report the sorrowful memory of her fallen friend.

Music reminds me of church, music reminds me of temple, only music is better because God isn't dead once you turn the sound up. My classmates and I are excited for rhythmic movement. We take off our shoes and socks and place them in cubby holes before running and skipping to the marching chords of Mrs. Osorio's piano. We strike wood blocks and shake hand-painted castanets and run around the large room to get a feel for eighth notes, which we call running notes. Dotted sixteenth notes are skipping notes. Quarter notes are walking notes. Whatever the tempo, make sure it's *con brio*. That's the direction for walking down a Manhattan street.

I listen up. I am a-quiver in music. At my new regular school, a junior high school in Queens filled with third-generation American bullies, everyone is starting to look the same for the wrong reasons. Kids make fun of me for still wearing sweatpants and sometimes still shitting in them, but I know this is a phase that will pass. I used to have black friends in elementary school. In fact I was the odd white boy out and there was never any trouble, at least for me. But at my new school most of the students are white, and they like being mean to themselves, and mean to me. Why must they be mean to me? Why must anyone be mean to anyone else? I like to play volleyball but they bully me when I don't go for the spike, and besides, I shouldn't play sports. I must protect my piano-playing fingers.

I can't get out of Queens fast enough. I dream of moving to Manhattan, where youths are civilized, where all people are concerned only with Brahms, where there's nothing but music all day and late into the night. I make the first of many promises to myself to one day live in a modest apartment on Madison Avenue and Sixty-Ninth Street. I will live above one of the French boutiques where Ms. Osorio buys her delicate blouses.

After school I run home to practice and complete my bland yet challenging exercises in counterpoint. I'm careful not to use parallel fifths in my exercises, even though they are the basis for all of the guitar music I'm starting to love, even though they are the only sturdy sounding constructions. Breaking the rules is the only way to make theory interesting.

I write a haunting composition in A minor.

I weep.

Why am I crying at myself?

Because I am famous!

No, forget A minor. It's better to focus only on compositions in major keys. Mrs. Osorio told us that one can listen to brisk Haydn sonatas and never even know that melancholy exists in this life. But then Chopin's clamorous prelude in the key of E major, a supposedly happy key, causes me to weep. It's confusing to hear a vision of the world going by. It is the ninth prelude, always the ninth, just like the ninth Brahms-Handel variation, as though it's the last inning of the game. Chopin's ninth prelude makes me, I am sure of it, come down with a cold.

What the hell am I supposed to do now?

It is too late to be a prodigy and too soon to be an amateur.

My music classmates are 32-karat latchkey Manhattan kids. Many of them live in a building called the Dakota, which sounds savage and warm. I meet the neighbors of the late John Lennon. I meet college-aged girls interning for downtown installation artists, the grandchildren of the descendants of grandmothers who personally knew Chopin. These Manhattan superstars are a second family and like a family I adore and am repulsed by them at the same time. They have crazy money but they never talk about it. Their community crisis is the construction of a building that will ruin their building's view. They park in heated garages. They know the names of the druggists in their pharmacies. Their fridges are bare except for bow-tie mustards and old hard bread.

One Saturday morning, in the window of a record shop on Third Avenue, I see the album cover for Andrew Hill's *Grass Roots*. A black and white boy playing together in the springtime wood chips. The next Saturday morning, in the same record shop window, I see the album cover for Ornette Coleman's *This Is Our Music.* I don't hear Ornette's music just yet, but the title makes sense. I think he means our music, like everybody, but maybe he only means our music, we are black. I don't get that just yet. A few years later, I'll never forget it. But now, I wander off Third Avenue letting everyone know that this is our music.

Because whose music would it be, if not ours?

I go to recitals with my Manhattan classmates. I ride in Volvos on the West Side highway coming back from concerts at Lincoln Center and master classes at Alice Tully Hall. I see Mrs. Osorio's family name in the $2,499-and-under donor page in a Lincoln Center program.

My teacher is a donor. Vital to the arts.

I promise myself that when I grow up I will own a Volvo.

The first question I ask parents is if they know the E major, the Ninth Prelude. This is our music, I let them know, these are our grass roots, I tell them plainly, but they have no idea what I'm talking about, and think I'm overexcited. Just like I don't know if I'm supposed to be Jewish or Catholic, I don't know if I'm supposed to be from Manhattan or Queens, I don't know if I'm supposed to be white or black, especially because white kids make fun of me for having a black boy's name, and I don't realize, I never will realize, that everything has already been decided for me and I have no choice in the matter either way.

I know they know that this is our music, even if they don't realize it.

This is our music, I tell them, but rich ladies know better than me.

This is a piece by Debussy, I say, it's called *Nuages*, which means, in French, well, clouds is what it means. Clouds.

They don't care.

It's OK.

The descendants of Chopin own Debussy, not me, and they own the seasons as they are scored out by Vivaldi, canvassed by Kandinsky, and they own the water lilies at the Met, not me, not Monet, and not the water lilies themselves, delicate things dead long ago.

○

Every season it takes a lifetime for spring to arrive, and every week another lifetime for Saturday morning to come. Today is a special day. We're going to have an afternoon recital. It is a confusing day! So my father will drop me off in the morning, drive back to Queens, and I will have the lunch hour all by myself until Daddy returns uptown for the afternoon recital. A few hours in Manhattan all by myself! I plan to take a casual lunch at the old-fashioned sandwich shop on Lex and then mosey over to the Hallmark store on Third to browse the high-end magazines. I will sit at the counter with my grilled cheese and ginger ale reading my favorite novel, *When The Kissing Never Stops.* Then, I will enter the Hallmark store and turn the pages of *Vogue* and *Elle* with their women on parade—oh and there is *Parade*.

Well, at least that's my plan.

At the end of our group class in rhythmic movement, all of the Manhattan kids get their shoes and socks from the cubby holes and leave the building for lunch back at the Dakota. I stay behind to clean up after them. I often clean up after class. It's a natural thing for me to do. I like to serve. I clean up at home, too, so why not clean up here? It's important to be useful. It's important to be nice to people and be interested in what they have to say. The only way you will ever learn anything is by listening to what other people say first. If someone asks you a question about yourself, answer politely, and then ask them the same question about themselves. Now be quiet. They will talk longer than you did. See? You're smarter than you were before.

Suddenly I hear Mrs. Osorio's heels walking into the room. She sees me cleaning and tells me to cut that out—that's what the janitors are for. She takes my hand and leads me into the back room.

She says we're going to have our poetry reading.

I'm so excited.

The week before she gave me two poems: "A Woman Waits for Me" and "Out of the Cradle Endlessly Rocking." She told me to think about how we could set them to music.

It'd be like a rap song, there are so many words!

She is still leading me into the back room, the service exit, but first I see a small urban garden. Butterflies spend quality time levitating above the flowers in this service entrance garden. It is a beautiful place.

In the back room there are a few tables and wooden chairs, a chalkboard with permanent staves, an old grand. I sit on the leather-cushioned stool. Mrs. Osorio places a wooden chair in front of me and sits on it. I face her, not the ivory piano keys. I feel bad for the elephants when I press down those keys, I feel bad for the cows when I sit on the leather stool, and I feel bad for the trees that made Mrs. Osorio's wooden seat.

"Did you read the poem, Tyrone?"

"Please call me Ty."

"Did you read the poem, Ty?"

"Yes, five times," I say, watching her pinkies, fingernails painted red. Then I close my eyes. I can't see her blouse anymore. I want to believe it's the same blouse from her Madison Avenue parcels.

"Did you read the right poem, Ty?"

"About the musical shuttle?"

"No, about the woman who waits for you."

"Yes. I read both. Five times. Five times in a row. I loved the poems. I need poetry to survive."

"You read about the woman who waits for you."

"I did. The woman who waits for me desires nothing."

"What did you think about the woman who waits for you?"

"I loved her. All five times. I loved her more and more. More and more and more. I love the poem so much. I will dismiss myself from impassive women."

We locate the text. We read the poem together. We make it a call and response. The poem is catechism, teaching me new sacraments. This is what I've been waiting for. I am becoming part of a radical sequence. I am worshipping at the altar of new faiths. Maybe I will get a tattoo. A piercing. Maybe I will dye my hair. Maybe now that I'm going to have sex with a woman I can have sex with a man, too. Maybe I can have sex with the black boy on the cover of *Grass Roots* and we will be so close to each other so as to become one person, and end this horrible separate business forever. Where does he live? Maybe I can have sex with everyone in the whole world.

"What does the woman who waits for you want?"

"Sex."

"Why?"

"Because all would be lacking if sex were lacking. Do you think we should set the poem to music? There are so many words, but I can do it. I think it should be in E major, the saddest happy key. Like my ninth prelude, I mean Chopin's, not mine, sorry. Like the final movement of the *Unfinished Symphony*. Like Op. 109."

"You could set it to music," Mrs. Osorio answers, wetting her palm and returning her hand to my erection which is hurting, pulsing, no foreskin but the sensitivity good.

"Who is this woman who waits for me?" I ask coquettishly. I know the answer to my question.

"I am," Mrs. Osorio says, and right then my penis grows even more. How excited I am, my penis all a-shiver, to hear the answers to questions I never needed to ask. "I am the woman, Ty. I am the woman who waits for you."

"Do you desire sex? Because all would be lacking if sex were lacking."

Of course it is not my penis that shivers but my whole body shivering when I learn my penis is connected to the rest of it. In temple I offer my body, in church I offer my body, I offer my body at the doctor, on the playground, I offer my body at school. This is another one of those offerings. Mrs. Osorio alternates licking the top of the penis and making herself wet by gulping down her own fingers. Even her fingers seem to be a blouse, rustling in the afternoon breeze blowing through the garden. I am in that room, astride that garden, until suddenly, unbelievably, Mrs. Osorio finishes, removes herself from me and orders me to clean my body and mouth in the janitorial shower upstairs.

I walk up to the attic of the cold building.

It's dark up there and the lights don't turn on.

I rinse off in the shameful dark.

And now I can hear the families down below, including my father, re-arriving for the afternoon recital.

I never went to lunch! My exciting lunch all by myself. Would I have paid the extra dimes for sliced tomato on my grilled cheese? I'll never know. I feel bad for the cow who made the milk to make the cheese. I feel bad for the vine from which the tomato was plucked. But I'm not hungry, anyway. The idea of human food repulses me, more than it repulses Gregor Samsa. Now that I've been fucked, I want a cigarette. And not the candy cigarettes my father rewards me with after a good day at the piano. I want the cigarette that will slowly kill me.

○

The recital room is packed with students and parents. I am the best piano player in school, so that means I'm the last performer. This afternoon, I will play Chopin's Prelude in E major. This magical piece of music. Others harp on the melancholy of the E minor, but I'm wise enough to know this is where the real sadness is at. The E major. As though a clock that does not tell time is ticking. Briefer than "The Sounds of Silence." I don't think I can play the piece, but Mrs. Osorio told me I could play my favorite piece if I worked very hard. And I did work hard. More than any other time in my life. For weeks I logged practice hours in my reporter's notebook. I wondered at the end of each day what I learned, if the work I did was any good, what I retained, how much I would forget, where I would start all over again tomorrow.

I stand up from the chair next to my father. I rise the small step onto the platform stage, sit in front of middle C at the baby grand. There's the usual applause from parents, and the coughs that catch in an audience's throat right before serious music begins. I declare that I must wait for complete silence. Actually, that's never going to come. And so I begin the prelude. Instead of taking it too fast, which is usually the case with live performance, I start very slow, almost at the tempo of sludge. There is an element of sludge to the E major, and in fact it may be one of the earliest examples of the romantic desire to escape the world, to tune down and growl and slash your way through a violent piece of music. But there is strictness to sludge. A military pulse. One foot in front of the other, and then the other foot in front of that one. For the listener it marches by all too quickly. The performer, though, must beat on.

Only in the second and third bars do I realize this military pulse. By then, I'd played this piece thousands of times. How can there be something new? This prelude, which made me sick once before, is only a prelude to war, the greatest sickness. And I almost start to cry. And I fear that I will one day have to go off to war, that I will have to bear arms against another terrified young man and possibly kill him, all for the imponderable glory of our imaginary nations. What a pity that war will be taking me now, when I've just begun an exciting new phase in my relationship with Mrs. Osorio. I do not want to go to war. I am just like poor Menoetes, the cattle-herder killed near the close of the *Aeneid.* Menoetes the peaceful boy who did not want war, but war would be his fate. A boy who, like me, is a stranger to all the gifts of the soil, who, like me, has a father who tills his crops on rented land, the land in my Daddy's case being the Dow Jones Industrial Average.

I will not escape war. It will come for me. Pain will come for me. Division is chomping at the bit. And I start to panic. I steal a glance over my sheet music at Mrs. Osorio. Her eyes are closed, hands folded in her lap. She is trying to feel the music I'm making.

Perhaps she is remembering the interlocking moisture of what we shared today. My speed picks up! Now I'm playing too fast. I fumble through the trills in the left hand, hitting multiple wrong notes, and that's when I really begin to cry. I can't play anymore and I pour tears. Parents mumble. Mrs. Osorio leaps up from her chair. She drags me into the same back room which had been the scene of our poetry reading. My father races into the room and takes me in his arms. It is the fastest, since Mommy died, that I've seen my father run. I'm so glad Mommy isn't here to see this. I'm so glad Mommy is gone so her ugly sickness won't ruin the beauty of my Saturday afternoons. Now I am *really* crying, it must still be for her, and I'm making all kinds of needless movements, kicking my feet in their uncomfortable dress shoes, flailing my arms out of my white shirt, pulling at my dark tie. Weeping violently. Exactly what I didn't want to do.

"Do not be so fearful," my father yells.

"I am going off to war," I stammer.

He laughs roundly. I accuse him of not being fearful—I use his word—of my inevitable deployment. "Daddy I don't want to go to war. I want to go back to Queens."

"Okay, okay," he shushes me, and himself, because he is also being loud.

Mrs. Osorio stands in front of the audience and apologizes for the scene. I am further humiliated that she doesn't stick up for me. My father and I are asked to leave through the service exit, beyond the urban garden, the long walk back to our Buick.

At the candy store on Lex, Daddy bribes me with a box of candy cigarettes.

"You want filtered or non-filtered, Tyrone? Slims or 100s?"

"Please don't call me Tyrone. I want both."

I laugh, I say yes to everything, I never say no, and stuff almost a whole pack of candy cigarettes into my mouth. And I blow some bubbles. Chew on it. I chew a few more. I swallow it all. I do anything people want me to do. They want me. They always do. People want me for me, that's the scary part. Especially when they're in a position to shape my thinking. I think I'm making a friend, exchanging ideas, when really, my body is the idea.

My body is all I have.

O

At my Junior High I'm challenged to an after-school fight by third-generation American bullies. Mean white men are going to beat me, their brother, to the ground. At first I refuse to fight. It's the wrong decision. It's only going to make things worse. I'm big for my age even at that age. I can take these bullies, I think, and punch them with my closed fist. But I can't do it. I can't raise my hands. I can't even close my fist. I dream of a man who cannot make a fist. Am I a pacifist or just a coward? I dream of a future story: one day I will perform a romantic feat that will make a woman who thinks I'm a coward realize I'm the strongest man she knows. I don't want to cause violence, shed blood, grant divorce. At synagogue, I read a mediation by a man who dreams of *a human creature unable to shed blood.* I dream of that human creature, too. At church, I hear the warning: *turn the other cheek.* I dream of dancing cheek to cheek with that cheek. And I say so, all of those things, to my youthful attackers—we can improve mankind! we don't have to waste it!—I say these things I don't even understand to the kids standing in front of me with their fists up. In their anger I see that my solitude is not going to make things easy for me. In their anger

I see only a glimpse of what is causing them enough pain that hurting me is the best activity they can come up with. Why are they blaming me for losing a volleyball game? Even this little fight I need to turn into the history of mankind. I have no sense of context, especially during conflicts. The fight quickly becomes unfair. I am pinned to the gated window of a jewelry store on the corner of Justice Avenue. Some of my best friends are taking turns making me cry. The store is closed, the gems removed from their window slots, but there's one ring that a lazy jeweler forgot to lock away, a green stone set in a gold band. I watch that stone and suffer my punishment. It probably is my fault we lost the game. I promise to never lose another game again. I didn't set the ball, I should have, why did I not stand up for my teammates, why did I go for the spike?

Those from the mob who were my closest friends call my house phone later that night and apologize for what they did. *Carried away, got out of hand,* fake words spoon-fed by parents. One boy was forced to repeat his father's conclusion that it was a *mob mentality.* How original. A mob mentality. Do you mean the wisdom of crowds? I've been in a lot of crowds, and never found wisdom in any of them.

o

I have twenty-two years of experience. My final year of college. I play music in high school and then I get a music scholarship to City College in Queens. I can't get out of Queens, it contains me. I still live at home with my Dad, who I never call Daddy anymore, and all of my Manhattan friends left NYC for college—SUNY Purchase, Brown, Oberlin, Boulder, Harvard: it all sounds like the same rich people shit to me. I'm stuck in Queens, and I'm so sick of music. I'd rather choke on a radish than listen to Chopin.

Wait a minute.

I taste slivers of white-hot radish careening down my throat.

It's the end of the fall semester. I'm walking with Professor Peter Gross toward the English building. Peter's asking about the tattoo on my arm. I show it to him.

"Deep," he says. "What does that mean for you, Ty?"

"Shame is sincerity leaving the body? Oh, it's my wayback definition of shame. Everyone needs one."

"I imagine many people do."

"Well, Peter," I say, always feeling weird to call my professor by his first name, "it was the first line of the first poem I wrote. I think it means that if you feel shame it's no big deal, you're just losing that part of you governed by an academic truth. You know? I want another one. Another tattoo. A cross above my heart. I used to want eighth notes on my shoulder, but not anymore. Everyone's getting them."

"You can't be buried as a Jew with tattoos," Professor Gross says.

"Oh I know. That's why I want the cross above my heart, so there's no chance, no matter what happens to me, that I'll be buried as a Jew anyway."

○

Everyone loves Professor Gross. I think he loves me more than anyone else. We kind of look alike, not tall, not short, widow's peak, which Peter terms the saddest hairline, lashes long and blueblack, brows soft and dark brown. I'm broad-shouldered, hard-stomached, trimmest, at my army weight. There's a war but I'm not joining. I'm cold-hearted, feverish, obsessed with girls and money—sweet, homely, good, patient, careful, thoughtful, sensitive like a monk, never judging, the happiest person many people know. I read too many books and work out a lot. Professor Gross is double my age but still at his army weight, a waist-size below Fahrenheit freezing. I shop at the GAP, maybe Banana Republic on Pell Grant check-cashing day. But Peter shops at those vaguely British supply company stores downtown which offer only store credit in their return policy. He lives in the city, in the East Village near Russ & Daughters. He wears a canary yellow shirt. It works for him, and yellow usually doesn't for guys like us. We don't want to be white, but we are, so we must try harder. We're both southern Italian Jews, that makes us Ashkenphardic-Sicilian, maybe? We're both olive-skinned, but what is olive skin? The color of an olive's meat-licked pit? Do we deserve, along with everything else, the olives too?

These are pressing questions as afternoons turn to evening and we lounge in Peter's office playing parlor games, turning random pages in unreadable novels and mocking what we find. There's something more to Wing Biddlebaum's fragrant hands than what Sherwood Anderson was thinking. There's something more to every man. And we find the best description of the weird thing our smiling eyes do on the first page of Thomas Hardy's *Far From the Madding Crowd*: "When Farmer Oak smiled, the corners of his mouth spread till they were within an unimportant distance of his ears, his eyes were reduced to chinks, diverging wrinkles appeared round them, extending upon his countenance like the rays in a rudimentary sketch of the rising sun."

"Holy shit," I say. "Not sure how I feel about the chinks."

"Delete the chinks," Peter says.

"But why the hell are we knocking ourselves out? We're not Ashkenphardic-Sicilians, we're just Farmer Oaks."

"Indeed. One day, Ty, you too may have a countenance."

O

I should be going to band practice, but I'm more interested in running into Peter. I'm barely stoned, by myself in the cold seminar room, blackening the whiteboard with lines from our favorite poems, searching for patterns that will snap the poems back together.

One needs to be very strong to love solitude.
One must have a mind of winter.

Professor Gross walks into the room. He stands at the whiteboard and reads my poem. He adds a line of his own:

Freed from shame, human growth is easy.

"That's good. What else you got?"

"You're stoned, Ty."

"I'm not," I lie. "I'm crying. My tears are too many for one man. If there's no poetry, nothing happens."

"I never know what to say to you when you're stoned."

"You don't have to say anything."

Now I'm down on my knees. Professor Gross can't see me. Now I do have a countenance. I authorize the breaking of poems.

Peter enters my body. This is what we had planned all along. This is what we were waiting for.

"Oh! If the world is too much with us, life slips by like a field mouse."

"That's a good one," Peter says. "That's a good one, Ty."

My teacher is inside of me. Reading comprehension. My teacher tells me I can do it, if I never stop. He has the hands of Wing Biddlebaum, the heart of Leopold Bloom, Humbert Humbert's halitosis.

"My mother waits for me," I say. "I am alone, with her, in a future April."

"Not bad."

"What else?" I ask.

"You're clenching," Peter says.

"I know. I'm stuck."

"Just breathe."

"Will someone just put a cock in this bitch and shut her up."

"That's better."

"At the essential landscape stare, stare at the dresser of deal."

"Good one. Let go," Peter breathes. "You're still clenching. You're acting like your father is here, Ty. Your father isn't here."

"I can't do it," I say. There's no new man, no altar, no radical sequence, no sacraments. Give me what I want. I will never be happy. A man who has failed men is coming.

O

Life is more complicated than it should be. Life should take place in lobbies, soft gray lobbies, small table, black-shaded lamp. Above the black lamp, a black Rothko. Let's have sex with a lobby.

The thirst to obey, wash, paint, sweep, prepare, serve, and get penetrated by a lifeless foyer. That hurts, hallway. But do it to me. Do it to me anyway. Turn me out, hallway, until I don't remember my name anymore, and when you've had enough, leave your hot load in my mouth.

My practice is developing, although I don't practice much. I'm extremely interested in future sex, the new combination of bodies, the orifices yet to be discovered. Let's look at those bodies. Let's see what warmth they bring us. How do we turn out a third being if the first two are still available? The recombination of sexual bodies. The rewiring of nature. Tell me about it.

Peter knows all about it. He knows what a radical sexual being I am. In fact, like Mrs. Osorio, he's helped me rediscover this true side of me. We have our own language. Let's fancy ourselves something. Let's call our classmates contemporaries, let's call books tomes, let's call Flushing Meadow the Forest of Arden and like Orlando from *As You Like It* staple poems to trees. Let's call an eggplant-colored couch an aubergine divan and let's read old-fashioned novels, very old-fashioned novels, very, very old-fashioned novels, very, very, very, old-fashioned novels, or let's read only free radicals, *Visions of Cody*, *In Memoriam to Identity*, *Opus Pistorum*, *The Dreaded Comparison*, *The Gulf War Did Not Take Place*, staple-bound magazines, reviews, gazettes and forums, and pair them with stinky cheeses, local soppressata, splay the stoneground crackers on a leaf-shaped serving tray with an acorn circle for dip.

Sounds good.

The men I believe in are kind, honest, hiding nothing, every man I meet, no matter his routine, no matter his reps, must be this way. Peter believes in men. He believes in the novel. He eggs art on. He thinks real life is nothing less than what you do every day. *Real life is what you live every day.* Real life can be anything you want it to be, if you never stop, don't you ever stop and start praising your own collapse.

But I do stop. And praise my own collapse. I'm failing out of my music classes and it feels good to admit to myself what a loser I really am. There are three things to be: appreciator, artist, technician—pick one and carry on, but I must be all three and at the same time. Plus, I'm paranoid. Every lip I read or snatch of dialogue I overhear I misconstrue as my contemporaries gossiping, like they have nothing better to do, about how I've given up. I'll just charge ahead and give up. I explain this to my contemporaries but they have no patience for my scattered emotions, tell me I can do whatever I want. Only next time, give them advanced notice if I'm punking out, so they have enough time to locate a sub.

"You don't understand," they say. "Art is hard work, like anything else." They avoid me, and then, suddenly, unbelievably, Professor Gross seems to do the same. He doesn't wait for me outside the music building. He doesn't return my calls. He won't lounge and chat with me in his office after his office hours are officially over. While I was waiting to turn out the hallways of the future I lost track of my man. He was standing right behind me.

Feeling like I must do something, I make an official office hours appointment to return the books I borrowed. I carry them with me in my book bag and unload them on Peter's desk. My back aches, even after the weight is gone. Peter eyes me with suspicion, counts the volumes by tapping the spines of each one. He's such an asshole.

"Where are the bookmarks?" he asks.

"You said I never needed to return them. Like Kafka. There's no need to return."

"You are not Kafka, Ty. But now that you're here, I'm wondering where the bookmarks are."

Does he really want his keepsakes from Brentano's, Shakespeare and Co., Posman, Barnes and Noble and St. Mark's Books? And Argosy's on Fifty-Ninth Street, Green Apple in San Francisco, Myopic in Chicago? Peter has too many books. Peter has too many bookmarks. He has toured the world and found nothing but placeholders.

"I burned the bookmarks," I say, and I go to leave his office. On my way out I bump into a new boy running in. We smile at each other, we're both cute. This boy is not olive-skinned, nor Farmer-Oak-Ashkenphardic-Sicilian. He's not at his army weight, even thinner, a POW yearning, a pale skinny white boy who grew up on Long Island listening to punk on purpose, helping his Dad waterproof a deck.

Peter stands up to greet him.

It becomes clear to me that Peter and this boy are going to take a walk and I'm not invited. But I follow them out of the English building anyway. When we walk by the Music building, Peter says, "Don't you have to practice, Ty?"

I shake my head.

Boy do I shake my head.

We leave school grounds, walk the service road perimeter of our precious college. I feel ridiculous. Boy do I feel ridiculous. Professor Gross and the young boy hold books of contemporary poetry. They are new books of contemporary poetry. They are very new books of contemporary poetry. They are very, very new books of contemporary poetry. They are very, very, very new books of contemporary poetry. I assume I'm lagging behind but really the two of them just sped up. Professor Gross points to one of the elms lining the boulevard. He says to me, "Ty, why don't you go make that tree. Could you do that? Do you think you could make a tree?"

Professor Gross is not merely asking me to make like a tree and leave. He is asking me to create the tree which will hasten my departure. I don't know what to say. All I can think is, yes, good sir, but where do I find the shears? How do I massage the roots? What is the first thing a man must do to make a tree? Should I find a water source? A hose?

I'm still so anxious, trembling scared.

Let me look down at my jeans.

Wretched, the fade of my denim.

Sometimes you look at your jeans and realize no one understands you.

I want to tell Peter everything. I want to be this man who can speak his mind, brash vocals, free of jugular clamps. I don't want to listen to you, I want to speak, and I want to scream at Peter, tonight you will be the figure in my dream. You will be my object. You will be my subject. You will be an engraving curtain, a curtain covering me. The two of us went through something immense, even if you don't think so. I will exaggerate your standing in my lucid dreams to prove to you how much I care. Even if you aren't in my dream tonight I will lie to you in the morning and maybe the weight of my lie will bear so heavy on my unconsciousness that later on this week, when the lights go out, you will appear, electric and sold. There is nothing more I want than our names sparkling on jazz and tap toes. I want to write a book of sayings all about the power of male friendship, a book too long and too heavy to be held by one man. I want to lend every man this book and say, that's okay, my friends, there is no need to return it.

○

I meet Jenny Marks in Peter's senior seminar, *The Autobiographical Fallacy.* Jenny is enrolled, I'm only auditing. We always leave class together, seemingly by accident. For a few weeks we sit in her car, a two-door Civic she calls Big Red. We chain smoke Parliaments with the windows up and listen to "Inbetween Days" on Saturday night. We listen to "Close to Me" and get closer to each other.

Jenny Marks wants to be an autobiographical fallacy writer. Well, she's already a self-obsessed chain-smoking hallway depressive who never wants kids. We've been at the same college this whole time but somehow we only meet at the end. It's one of the many things Jenny and I never get tired of talking about. And it turns out we went to the same junior high school, even though we never ran into each other. I wonder if Jenny cheered on the boys who were always beating me up.

She lives with her parents in Corona, like me, and she's a third-gen American, like me, a Catholic Jew, like me, who went to Catholic high school in Queens and then remained in Queens for college. She isn't ashamed of living with her parents—in fact she loves Queens, never wants to leave. She doesn't have a thick white New York accent. It's all the reading she does. Unlike me or my father or family members who left Queens for Northern New Jersey or South Florida, Jenny sounds like a normal white person.

"You're beautiful, Ty, can I come over?"

"I'm supposed to say you're beautiful."

"I know I'm not."

Jenny's no snob, but she is full of herself. She's been out of New York only once—Disneyworld. Dragged there in tears, she left with a smile on her face. "Orlando, Ty, is possibly the scariest place on earth. They're more full of themselves in Orlando than they are in Brooklyn."

Her lips are small, chapped year-round, wine-blistered, even when she hasn't had any. She wears white uptowns, gray sweatshirts and baggy, paint-stained jeans. I always see paint on her clothes but I never see her painting.

"My clothes are old," she says. "But none of my new paintings are any good."

Her long hair, she's been messing with it. She's been biting it again, pulling it out, roots thirsting like a neglected plant. She's not sure if she should cut her bangs or grow her bangs. She doesn't like it when they grow so long she gets wings.

She owns a hot pink Stratocaster, plays the intro riff to "Come As You Are."

"Learn the chorus," I tell her. "It's not that much harder than the verse."

"Teach me, Tyrone. What kind of name is Tyrone for a meathead?"

"My mother loved Tyrone Power," I say.

"I'm sorry about your Mom. Why didn't your Dad get married again?"

"I don't know. I can't figure out why my Dad does anything."

Jenny stole a flute from her elementary school. I find it under her bed.

"You should clean out under here. I mean, I just found a flute."

"Why clean?" Jenny answers, squeezing a pillow between her legs. "So the monsters can fit? I hate this temptation we have in Queens to clean out under our beds and tell the multigenerational saga. That's what Manhattan wants from us. I love my parents, Ty, but that's not who we are. Let them deal with themselves on their own time."

"Yeah but don't you want to get an apartment in the city?"

"No, why would I do that?"

"To stop being indebted to your parents?"

"I can do that while I still live here. You live with your Dad."

"Yeah but I take care of him."

"Well, I take care of my Dad, too."

The free rent helps. Jenny fails to keep a job as a waitress, soggy dumplings in the German restaurants behind the cemeteries. She's got unlimited hope, my girl, prone to insecurity-fueled outbursts like her father, her mother, her sister, her brother, her aunts on both sides, her cousins, her friends, me. We're all a mess. All the parties we go to are on the Lower East Side or in Brooklyn. We spend long hours on empty trains back home. We spend a lot of time sitting in Big Red. We spend a lot of time taking the train into the city for no reason at all. We joke that one day we'll get all the LES and Brooklyn kids to move to the Big Q, or we'll get secure enough that we don't have to run to them every time they throw one of their famous parties.

I invite Jenny over. I am beautiful. I have to hold back. Her breasts are soft and big, nipples white-red, invisible. She has no ass, boxy shoulders, a hot tongue. I record to tape Monk's "Ask Me Now" and "Pannonica" because they don't come after each other on the CD. These modern jazz compositions are strip-show decay. Jenny rides me and I look away to keep still, stare at the poster of

Monk on my wall, a reproduction of his *Time* magazine cover I cut out of a collector's issue of *Rolling Stone*. Jenny clumps my chest hair in her fingers, licks the birth scar on my lip where no hair grows. I look away, stare at the poster of Monk.

Jenny becomes my lifetime with Monk: I love it, but I've been hearing it forever.

"You're so beautiful Ty."

"Is that all you care about?"

"My meathead. You're my big beefy meathead. My big beefy beautiful meathead."

"Who's your favorite artist?" I ask.

Jenny tells me about Lee Lozano, who locked herself in her Manhattan walkup for months. She wouldn't take visitors. She wouldn't go out into her hallway. We know all about it. Lee sketched vaginas, cocks, balls and a doorbell that's ringing—*bell stop ringing*.

"Nice," I say. "Like, it's not a pipe. You know, this is not a pipe, but it is a pipe." I need to sound smart in front of Jenny, make humanistic connections. Otherwise, I feel lame.

"It has nothing to do with pipes," she says.

"I'll read you a poem."

"My meathead."

I reach under my bed. I still have the print-out of "A Woman Waits for Me" from Mrs. Osorio. I keep it with my pornos.

"Whatever," Jenny says when I'm done. "I never agreed with this poem. I learned from it not to agree with it."

"Then it meant something, at some point, right? You had to know it to not agree with it."

"I guess. It's patriotic. It's chauvinistic. Plus, it's gay."

"Like you mean, let me go to war and do man-things while Jenny Marks, my woman, waits for me, all sad and tremulous."

"Yeah. Go read your gay poem about women waiting for you with Professor Gross."

Jenny comes closer. We're under the sheets. We've been there for days and we're going under the sheets even further. She says, "your woman doesn't need to wait for you no more."

O

After sex, we get so hungry. We leave my bed and drive to the diner during a drizzle. We share a twenty-dollar hamburger deluxe. Now it's pouring outside. We could wait it out, but we want to tell each other we love each other during the downpour.

"I love you," I say, but a part of me isn't sure.

"I love you too, Ty," Jenny says, but a part of me isn't sure.

We go on in this way for what feels like forever, until, right before graduation, things suddenly change. It used to be that Jenny and I didn't need plans unless she made plans elsewhere. Now she seems to be doing that more and more.

One Sunday I go looking for her in the city.

"What have you been doing?" I ask when I find her in the diner on Fifty-Seventh Street, an endless cup of coffee and her journal of 128-pages. "What have you been doing this whole week?"

"Accumulating receipts. I needed to be alone."

"Let's eat? Maybe?"

"I just ate. Am I even hungry again?"

"Maybe not. I guess I'm not. Not really."

"Let's get something, though," she yawns. "Let's go somewhere else."

"Am I boring you?"

"No, I'm just hungry. I always yawn when I'm hungry."

"I thought you just ate."

"Let's go back to Queens," she says.

We're standing in front of Carnegie Hall. I remember the joke I always let my father tell—*How do you get to Carnegie Hall? Practice.* But I don't practice anymore.

We're standing on the corner of Fifty-Seventh Street and Seventh Avenue and I think I can see up and down the whole avenue, up and down the entire history of my dreams. Downtown, I see the hospital where the village bohemians got sick nervous and died, and the awning of the Village Vanguard, an awning photographed for album covers, an awning I know exists. And across the street from the Vanguard the short fence of colorful tiles dedicated to 9/11 dead—the day President Bush called The Day of Fire—with matchbook-ready questions like, "Why didn't we get to say goodbye?" And further uptown, the pissy mystery of Times Square, where all of Rufus Scott's problems start in *Another Country.* And uptown, on the Upper West Side, the aging thinkers tossing and turning like Mr. Sammler, the old man who feared he went off to sleep and woke up in the morning reading the wrong books, the wrong papers. And right in front of us in Carnegie Hall, against time, the foreign man who escaped music like I did, who escaped the orchestra and broke through the death strains of Mahler's Ninth, waving his arms from the no-admittance fire escape, because he had to live his life outrageously, from those rickety fire escapes, and if he were going to die that night then let him die outside, in the open air, not fall to his death to Mahler's dying strains while seated quietly, privileged, stadium-tiered, in the red plushness of the intimate concert hall. I'm telling Seventh

Avenue all of this, I'm telling Jenny all of this, she's nodding and she's yawning at me because she's on her own thing that she never says out loud. Jenny never says what she's thinking out loud because her thoughts are always changing. But mine, Seventh Avenue, stay the same. Seventh Avenue and its whores chained to the adrenaline drip in my head. Strict composition. No self-pity. The courage to let go of what's lost. The relationship between the composition and the self-pity. Schoenberg's praising of Webern's devotion to his commandment that in order to achieve pure concentration you must remove yourself from self-pity. A huge problem, self-pity, the natural bend to false modesty, forcing yourself out of bed, catching the hours when the spirit is waning, which is the time for the sequencing of togetherness. Webern's question about *Das Lied von der Erde.* The possibility that the work was too beautiful, too much, too personal, and how he felt humbled to the point of asking whether he was entitled to hear the work at all.

"Should I go on?" I ask Jenny.

"I think you can stop."

You know what I mean about Seventh, though. The Seventh is all."

I look over at her. She's finishing up a big yawn.

"I can't be around you right now Ty."

"I'll shut up. I promise. You talk. I'll think about what I want to say while you talk, but I'll never say it."

She says she can't talk. She says she's not hungry, she's sure of it, she's going home and getting into bed. She runs away from me, down to the R train, and leaves me standing on Seventh Avenue all alone.

O

At graduation my father takes photos of me with my arm around Professor Gross. Peter tells Dad I'm prompt and courteous. If only all students could be like me. I went on humiliating myself by auditing Peter's classes. I even graded student essays for him, because being a professor is such hard work. I gave myself the B-minus I deserved. I gave Peter's new boyfriend an A+.

I know that after today I'll never see Peter again. I brought his bookmarks—I even found the ones from Powell's in Portland—but when I go to return them he tells me there's no need.

"I'm no Kafka," I tell him.

"That's very true, Tyrone. We don't want you losing your place."

It's a warm sunny morning in late May. I sit, with Jenny, in the last row of the student section. Our hearts beat fast and tears come to our eyes after every decent turn of phrase. During the commencement speech, from some kind of survivor of a hurdle that's not mine, I forget everything I learned in college, every conversation I started, contributed to, heard or overheard. Every chord I played, book I read, I'm no longer interested. I want to become Jenny's meathead, or further improve upon that dimension of my personality, get married, want kids if she does, work hard, get money, buy gear, fancy face wash, get out of Queens and move to Manhattan.

Maybe. I don't know.

We hear the voices of other students around us:

"I don't think anyone who goes to school here actually thinks they're going to graduate."

"It's like four more years of high school living with your parents."

"Or five."

"Or six."

"This is seven for me and I still need to take gym in summer school."

"Me too."

"Me three."

"What year is it?" I ask Jenny.

"2003.144444444444444...."

The ceremony finally ends. Jenny and I go meet our friends on the grassy hill behind the amphitheater. Fifty kids sitting on a slope. I recognize almost all of them. These kids, this hanging out, I realize it was my real education. I don't pretend to speak for people other than myself but today is the one day I can make a speech, and I'm thinking: Our important contribution to the perpetuation of fascism will not go unnoticed, graduates! We deny and claim birthplace at the same time. Do we achieve? No we squander, committed to false starts, searching for perfect takes. Borough of unplanned children, my barebacked brothers. What difference we will make is unknown. There is no reason for us to be innocent. Every single day is the start of our less innocent life. What we are is guilty. And we have not even begun to discover the power of our guilt. Whatever we say, we say exactly what we mean, and lose our sincerity as we would like others to lose theirs. The guilty rule, and we are the guilty rulers, a stoned alliance, a godless herd.

Mainstream

If I speak in the tongues of men or of angels, but do not have love, I am only a resounding gong or a clanging cymbal.
— *1 Corinthians 13:1 (NIV)*

That summer I go nowhere. Others return. Jenny and I see each other, but less and less. She says she is too sad to see anyone, even me. She doesn't return my calls. I come to realize that's the main reason I'm making them. I find it difficult to be alone, can't bear it, solitude is ill. I pull life down to hold on to it, I push life away. Memories are so heavy, though, that it doesn't take long for pushing and pulling to engage the same muscles.

I am not broken up about our breakup so much as unbearably whole, attached to our memories. If Jenny won't call me back I'll go to her. Or near her. I walk her streets but I'm scared to actually arrive on her block, so I walk home. Her family is crazy. I call her. She won't call me back. I don't sleep. There's too much to think about. Maybe I get a hood rat to come over. As long as I buy condoms, my Dad is cool with me sleeping with anyone I want in his house. Out of a politeness that's more a habit than a guiding principle, I ask the hood rat to stay the night. She says, "I don't stay over, don't you know I'm a hood rat?" She leaves, I still can't sleep. Insomnia is having no place to rest your other elbow. I turn over on my other side and imagine a soundproof music room. Reeds, sticks, mallets, bows, melodicas and accordions. That's how I count sheep. Tom Waits defined the "gentleman" as someone who can play the accordion, but doesn't. I sit on my chair and do not play the accordion. I pick up a rosewood guitar and strum a day-old song. My parasites, my songs. I host, they consume, for glucose, nothing more. I don't want to hear. I don't want to listen. The sound I want to make is no sound. I need contemplation, I need to just wait, and waiting is the one thing I'm not allowed to do. I play yesterday's song. Another song about the future. Yesterday it sounded brilliant, so good, now its limitations are all I hear. Hookless plain repetitive boring junk. Only I know what I meant, and I don't mean it anymore.

Jenny finally calls. My father picks up. I rush to the phone.

"Only when it's convenient for her, Ty," Dad says. "Only when it's convenient for her."

She says she can come over, if I'm not busy, she'll bring a pot of boiled chicken. I'm not busy. We have sex on my bedroom floor, we eat the chicken. We have sex on my twin-sized bed, order Chinese wings from the grease spot on Justice Avenue. We try anal sex. It works. We watch *Le Souffle au Coeur*, *Un Coeur en Hiver*, *Boxing Helena*, we watch *La Notte*. We fall asleep. When we wake up we want zeppoles—a doughy, deep-fried pastry rubbed in powdered sugar—from Gino's Pizzeria, but just zeppoles doesn't meet the delivery minimum, so we order a small pizza and give it to my father. Dad eats the entire pizza and falls asleep in the living room. I open a bag of almonds and wonder when he's going to die.

"Every man wants his father to die," Jenny says. "You're not special."

"I didn't say I was. I don't want him to die, I just want to know when. The exact minute."

"Say it like in Salinger," Jenny requests.

"God dammit. I didn't say I *was*. I don't *want* him to die, I just want to know *when*. The exact *minute*, for Christ's sake."

"You can't. It's going to be sudden no matter how it happens."

I eat my almonds, think about how heart-healthy they are. "Well, I want to know the exact minute. I want to know the exact minute my father is going to die so I will be prepared to be alone in the world."

"I'm here, Ty. You don't have to wait for me anymore."

○

At night I turn the AC down to Lo Cool so I can sweat a little. July 4th comes and goes and now it's time to get a job. After a dozen failed interviews in advertising and related "creative" fields, I secure a position as a junior marketing strategist with a management consulting firm headquartered on Wall Street. It occurs to me that I have no real skills for this job and was only hired because I am a man, good-looking, a well-dressed white college grad, clean, personable, and filled with five-borough bonhomie. I get my first check and feel like a big shot. At the Fifty-Ninth Street station I see the staircase to the R train but I'm not going home, no way. Well, not yet. I go to Bloomingdales instead and handle a sweater that costs hundreds of dollars. When I feel this material I feel the man I am becoming. I charge over a thousand dollars of clothing on my Discover card, modern-fit pants and slim-fit shirts, two sweaters. A tiny bald man, measuring tape hanging down from his neck, tells me this jacket is versatile.

"You mean it goes with anything?"

"Anything. For work, a weekend getaway, whatever."

"I've never been on a weekend getaway."

"Buy this jacket and you will. Wear this jacket with your pajamas when you drift off to the land of Nod."

I buy the jacket. It has a removable lining I will never remove. I leave the store and walk out of my way to Madison Avenue so I can take the bus uptown. When I pass the French boutiques I think about Mrs. Osorio and wonder what she's doing now.

I'm not going home. Not yet.

O

Lexington Avenue is my anchor. From there I catch the train to Wall Street and the weekend train to Astor Place and points west in Greenwich Village. Rarely do I feel like the hero of my own life, a portrait of an age, but rather I feel like an abandoned child crawling across the floor of someone else's story. I am sleeping again, probably because being a strategist makes me so tired. Restful sleep every night and I wake up shameful of its ordinariness. Most nights I have easygoing dreams, nothing to suggest a significant mind: waving goodbye to friends, my father sticking his head out the window while I throw a ball against a wall. Or I'm seated in an upper Madison Avenue diner, wondering if I ordered the wrong toast. My mother develops like a photograph. My mother files photographs in a shoe box. My mother orders another coffee at the diner. My mother reads me a poem by William Carlos Williams. I pass a film actor on the street, tell him I also admire his stage work. Critics in my dreams are also stylists in their own right. The domestication of a drifter, one of a series. Or I am a young girl making concentrating-face while papa teaches me to fish. A lunch lady plops a patty onto my tray. I dream I hear snippets of dialogue from the *Superman* franchise, they fall out of my mouth like loose teeth. My dreams are a good reason to get out of bed in the morning and go downtown to work.

Sundays always feel like they're a week away, never more so than on Saturday afternoon. I put in long hours. In the evening I like to catch the R train at Rector Street in order to get back uptown. There's a quicker route home, but I like riding the local because I get a seat and watch my own reflection in the Queens workers staring back at me. I am a Queens worker too, but not like these chumps. They work six, seven days a week and have a second job, if they're lucky. They travel long distances to stuff my burrito and bus my tray. They are short men with bad clothes who believe they too deserve the night. They ache for storybook Manhattan, the slant of its swing, the power of its money, the glory of its girls. These assholes are mosquitoes for feminists, payday Lotto addicts scratching tickets with unlucky pennies. They bring twenty of these casino games on the train at Rector Street and lose everything by Chelsea. These men are homophobic, racist puppy dogs. I fear these men, stinking of poverty and horniness and on the verge of modern wildness. If they play the wrong video game they might access weapons and shoot up a subway car. I would die in another man's misinterpretation, another man's level up. On warm nights I walk all the way home in order to avoid these underground men.

The streets exist. People engage and watch where they're going. There is intersection, more than one way. I get around and I have to move around to do it. I do not observe. I do not take it all in. On any street I walk at a brisk pace. My college years are over and I am no longer allowed to stroll. I hate the idea of the man walking around making observations. Men even older than me, they still stroll, they observe and mute their auditory sense by

wearing headphones and they don't look where they're going as
they write down thoughts in their pocket notebooks, as if the city
needs a detailed chronicling of their detached maundering, peace
in the city because there's a break in their disillusionment and their
pleasurable urban comedy makes sense, like they're tilling some
kind of urban soil when men know better than anyone else that
everything is cultivated and nothing will grow. I am not one of
those young men. I walk and I get somewhere. I become obsessed
with destinations. And often I smile but not too much, because I
remember what happened back in the day. A happy couple strolling
on the Lower East Side. The girl was murdered. The murderer, also
female, told the police or she told the news—I'd come to believe
there was little difference between the organizations, I'd come to
realize the Constitution wasn't worth the parchment it was drafted
on, the preamble a track-changes suggestion which should've been
rejected—that she shot the girl because she didn't like the smile on
her face. The girl got shot because she had a smile on her face! So I
don't smile. I don't stroll. I'm not happy. And if I do smile on the
streets, because sometimes the beauty of the city begs you for it,
well, I check myself.

   I hear my voice. Dum-ta-dum. I'm a legendary sportscaster
only hardcore fans remember as a shitty player. I over-drill, burn
for my chest, puke for my cuts, I'm the quarterback and the nose
tackle crouching in front of my center. But I am also my father's
voice, the morning of my career-ending injury. I won't make it in
the game, I'll make it on the sidelines. I knot a color man's tie and
hang a look of sadness over my face whenever off-the-field antics
threaten the purity of the game.

   My middle toes bleed through sweat socks, this is hurting my
elbows more than building my triceps, and here come the knees. I

watch training videos, laminate swim routines, plyometrics, SEAL pushups, interval training. What am I training for? Compound drills are my secret. They're how I build muscle and burn calories at the same time. Squat and then raise up into an overhead press. Lunge and hold a bicep curl. But without a disciplined diet no compound move makes a difference. The six pack begins and ends in the kitchen.

I read poetry on my lunch hour. I fancy myself Frank O'Hara, only he worked in a museum and I work for management consultants. I tell myself both are concerned with value. Really, it's the same job, and art is the worst business of all. I am still interested in the angular poetry being published in small magazines. I spend my money to support these movements and it makes me feel good. This poetry is creatureless, characterless, drained of Plath—verse which could double as stage directions and screenplay prompts for a film that will never be produced. Everyone is really into disclosing who they are and I dig that, it's a sign of a healthy economy.

Jenny Marks and I visit the Alexander Rodchenko retrospective at the Modern and learn the early Soviet artist disapproved of the commodification of women. Rodchenko thought turning women into Parisian street products was a big problem with western-style capitalism. (This phrase is just peculiar to me. When I hear "western-style capitalism" I see a BBQ entrée, "capitalism" the substitution for "braised ribs.") For Rodchenko, women must be more than beautiful products. They are not high-end face wash at the drugstore. They are not items of exchange. Women are not the gift cards they trade with equanimity over Christmas.

I don't stalk women as individuals, I stalk their concepts. I lurk in areas where women transform themselves. I pace back and forth outside nail and hair salons, watching the ground, pretending I've lost my keys. I set myself up to be in situations where women are closing doors to be alone with other women, waxing and tanning, bronzing and tweezing. My barber is not the best, but he runs a spray-tanning booth as a side business and from my vantage point in his mirror I watch the sprayer leading her customer behind the spa doors. The woman emerges minutes later, glowing with prep, wet and orange and tropical, western-style.

I seek out the moments in a woman's day when she experiences what pain management handouts call "slight discomfort." An MIT student escaped from Cambridge wearing tasseled loafers, only her new loafers are too tight. The impediment that forces a nurse to remove her white shoe and lean against a mailbox to flick the pebble out of her sole. A runner at a greening stoplight is ready to resume jogging but, oh no, she has to itch below her knee. How a big watch won't rest on a thin wrist. A blonde scowls at me only to realize she left her sunglasses on the dashboard. A slow song at the end of the night which allows a woman to run away.

○

The city is every four hours. The city is an endless druggist. There is no sober circumscription. The drugstore itself becomes a kind of street. Here is where I will produce my questions. I walk in and out of the drugstores as though they are interconnected by pedestrian tunnels in an arctic land. I wear modern-fit clothing though my purpose is traditional. I approach a stranger as she scans the shampoo aisle in a drugstore. But before I approach her I must approach myself, make vanity checks in the mirror affixed to the reading glasses display and catch a good glimpse of her without being too obvious. Ideally, I can wait for the woman to make a vanity check to *her* face. Even casually dressed, shopping for shampoo, my kind of woman will hint at formal vanity, a remembrance of occasional energy that makes her feel, if only for an instant while idling her morning away in a shampoo aisle, that she is a silver starlet, wearing a designer gown and borrowed necklace rare and delicate enough to be insured, the cuts in her sculpted arms an impression, like the enchantments of old she is indeed a beautiful goddess, *bella dea*, her hair not in a maintenance twist but curled, full, flowing, the color expert. I look for this disguised moment the way Aeneas, who discovered Rome, knew his bare-kneed mother Venus by her walk. And already I feel like I'm going to pass out.

I take a big breath. I do not approach the shampoo-shopper unprepared. The items in my tote are chosen to produce certain effects. I think of the women I've known whose fathers have died. The aftershave is what they keep. Also in my tote, to signal good eating habits, a trio of bagged oranges, a boxed assortment of whole-wheat crackers, to suggest healthy, casual snacking. Lastly, a party item urgently needed, an item I could not forget. A box of birthday candles. A hint I am throwing a party for a wide circle of friends.

When I approach a stranger I must ask them a question. I can't pretend I'm an epic hero with a *bella dea* for a mother and she will recognize me, her *uomo di cultura*, her *uno vero romano*, even in disguise.

"Can I ask you an innocent question?" I say, and often, if I can concentrate, this question is asked in an even more old-fashioned diction, "might I ask," or "may I ask."

My ultimate goal? The difficult-to-say "may I ask you a question." To force it out of my mouth, to fight the habit of "hey" and "lemme." These diction exercises will save me from early-onset Alzheimer's, like holding my toothbrush in my other hand, or throwing a rubber ball a thousand times against a white wall, or that advanced stage of weight-lifting when I remember, in early and late repetitions, to lower my shoulders, squeeze my abs, or the most difficult thing to do under duress: breathe normally.

"May I ask you a question?" And if the woman says no, turns her head and walks away, I too walk away, burning with rage and rejection and jealousy, hatred of all women. Smoke burning deep in a pebble history, out of time, nuclear heat from the Crab Nebula, rage from thousands of years ago. I move on and get back out onto the street, back into time, find the nearest subway and brood it out. But if the woman answers "yes, you may," or, disappointedly, "yeah, I guess," I offer, in the form of a question, a light-hearted confession.

She carries a leather handbag. She wears a slouchy peach blouse and leopard-print flats. There is no discursive inking on the top of her foot. Her hair is long and straggly, in need of treatment, a new shampoo, one that repairs. Her corduroys are not the current fit.

Those cords, their datedness, spark my interest. And inspire my question. I must advertise an active mind, filled with ideas. A man in a casual hurry to get things done. A mind constantly trying to improve itself. A man who knows that contemplation brings no peace. I want to present myself as a man of goals. So I say to the woman in the loose-fitting cords, "Hello. May I ask you a question?"

"Yeah, I guess."

"Well, I'm a struggling watercolorist. Color is my thing. I'm wondering the particular shade of brown of your cords. I can see its name spinning on my color wheel. It's on the tip of my tongue."

"You're kidding."

"Not exactly. I am not a watercolorist. But who among us does not wish to retire from life and set up an easel facing the Mediterranean, capture the stillness of the brown sea?"

"Are you okay?" she asks. "Umber. Burnt."

"Burnt umber," I repeat, and I thank her and shake away, leaving my bagged oranges, birthday candles and aftershave at the register, prevarications never rung up. I don't even deserve my products. I forget the reason I entered the drugstore in the first place and escape through the automatic doors.

○

Reading the meandering, autobiographical, hyper-sexed novels of Edmund White is my favorite waste of time, even though all of the sex occurring in these novels is between men. The bearish details physically repulse me. But I crave the shamelessness in White's voice. Straight men, like me, hide their hope for men. Straight men have a do-or-dieness. *Hey, I'm just here for the establishing shot.* But White's men have a do-and-do, a do-si-do.

I want some of that freedom.

As a free man I can never get enough freedom.

Even though there are hundreds of men in White's novels, he is the only man. He never finds himself, like I do, split in two. Or his splits are something even further along which I can't even perceive. He is an indecent man. And he makes no elaborate, lyrical excuses for his caddishness. He stakes new claims on fidelity. He promises he never fantasizes about other men during sex, yet he admits that his mind would start wandering if he were ever forced to sleep with the same man every night. Then he'd have to fantasize about other men in order to stay hard. The prospect of that kind of disloyalty violates his code of bodily sincerity.

I acquire a similar code. Once I read about it. When I have sex with a woman I think of nothing but her. When we are alone our fluids are not being policed by technology. We lose focus by concentrating on sensational things. An affair lasts a whole weekend. Or even the whole of a work week. But by the following Sunday night I have to conjure different women to stay hard. So I have the same fidelity issues as Edmund White. When I read about them.

White's novel *The Farewell Symphony*. The book cover, a recumbent man puffing sexual bubbles up into a musical staff, catches my eye in the window of Mercer Street Books. The title grabs me because I get the musical allusion. The Haydn symphony where the players exit the pit one by one until there's no longer the possibility of music because the composer has said so. White used this musical allusion as a somber metaphor for his friends who had died, suddenly and in great numbers, of AIDS. This novel becomes a kind of bible. I do not use "bible" lightly. What I take for gospel in *The Farewell Symphony* is everything but its central message— loving and turning out other men.

White speaks of his compositional method of confession. A kind of weaving where the next thing weaved is shifted slightly off-center. I relate this to my understanding of Morton Feldman's musical compositions. His fascination with rugs. I relate to Feldman, a composer among painters because he was a straight man among mostly gay men, weaving his gay rugs. Edmund White's rugs are really throws. Runners. In his outpourings there is a quality distant from the sheltering attitudes and bombastic descriptivism of Feldman's poised art. Or at least White poised himself very still to make it seem that way. If it just happens to be in my bag, I will tell women about, or even read aloud to them from, the novel. I recite these hard and bearded druggy exploits of 1970s-and-beyond gay sex while recovering and preparing to leave their apartments. And of course I leave out the AIDS. The women I meet don't want to hear about AIDS. They express dissatisfaction and tell me, "turn off the faggots and go to sleep."

No, I'm leaving.

Now I'm the hood rat.

I rarely spend the night anywhere, preferring, I must admit, early morning walks back uptown and over the Fifty-Ninth Street bridge, one foot after the other through the shoring hour, when the world is too sleepy to judge.

O

I walk off the human path, follow purebred paw prints in the snowy park. I search for the underpass where Ed Norton gets beat up by his best friends in *25ᵗʰ Hour*.

Poor Ed.

I watch Ed Norton get beat up by Binghamton municipal workers in *Rounders*.

Poor Ed.

I watch Ed Norton get beat up in *Fight Club*.

Poor Ed.

The end of *Fight Club* lied. It suggested I would be two men. I would be the one to burn the buildings down and I would be the one to watch and smile from a building across the street. I would be two men, not one, and I would stand hand-in-hand with my lover and watch the structure crumble. But I don't get to burn the building down. It's burned down for me, and for my own good.

At work they judge my personality and the verdict is COOPERATOR. My descriptors are *modest, sociable, predictable, helpful.* I attend plenaries, a fancy word for meeting. I give up using asterisks in instant messages, write "fuck this shit" instead of the bullet-ridden "f*ck this sh*t." Obscenity, I learn, saves lives. I have a password to a subscription-only portal. I retrieve all sorts of cool metrics. It's a powerful tool once I figure out how to use it. There's a tutorial and a FAQ. What I'm trying to say is, there's documentation.

I'm a good co-worker, a good listener—strangers confess themselves and I give sympathetic, careful advice. What seems important goes by too fast, what's day-to-day takes more than a day to process. I am many things to many people—whatever they want, I agree. Maybe I muster a "come-on" but only with my head down and my eyes closed to conflict. At other times I can sense my day is on the line and I force the right words out of my mouth. Unless it's something I wish to be, I won't be anyone's fool.

From my desk I look out a sealed window onto Broad Street. So named because it is narrower than Broadway. An oversized American flag takes up most of the columnar real estate of the stock exchange, the day's IPO banner flies beneath. The bell rings and trading begins and I think of Lee Lozano's drawing and the plea to please, please make the bell stop ringing, please, please don't let anyone come up. But you can't wait. The bell is going to ring. In the early evening shadows, when the yellow marble of the exchange glows radioactive, I imagine the horse-riding cops have become ancient props, caryatids with smelly pits, propping the economy up.

O

My boss, or I call him my manager, Tweed Spreckman—the balls on this prick. Tweed draws me into the hiring process. He gifts me a Harvard Business School pamphlet for dummies: *How To Light a Fire Under Your Employees*.

"If you ever need to start a fire," he says, "just burn this shit."

He teaches me that hiring is a personal process. You hire the people you judge you will get along with as people, and those people never let you down.

We hire one woman, Krista Kaplan, just because she's hot. I'm charged with showing her the ropes.

Tweed and I ride the elevator. He wears a navy blazer with thirty buttons, loafers that make his small feet look like mahoganized pears. He is sixth-generation American, a towering figure, an inch taller than a slumping Prescott Bush. He holds his usual snacks: a soda the size of a flowerpot, turkey jerky, and a bag of corned pork. He is one of several men I report to who dresses like a golf spectator and eats like a truck driver. I have never met anyone like him before. Work turns out to be like the old joke about joining the army and traveling to distant places and killing people, only we don't kill people, not to their faces.

"This week sucks," Tweed says, pressing the lobby button. He says that every week.

"Oh yeah. Sucks."

"Shitcan this week," he says, and since we're in an elevator he forces me to deliver an elevator sales pitch for one of our service offerings. He sips from his soda and rips a new one to his corned pork. It looks like he's trying to hide his turkey jerky.

He lets me out of the elevator first. We stand in the lobby, our work-blank sex-starved eyes following prim accountants and peaceful interns.

"How's the home front," I ask. Tweed is the only man I know in his 40s. Child-bearing years. He has three kids, the eldest five. They show in his belly. He lives on Long Beach, Long Island, where his wife's family and her family's family is from. Tweed thinks Long Beach is made up of trash, his wife not necessarily an exception to the rule.

"You'll find out about home front," he answers. "Enjoy being homeless while you can. When you get married, you feel like Phil Jackson. Four years later, you're Tim Floyd. You don't meet new women anymore, unless you're an ass. All you want to do is suck their ankles when they pass you on the street."

"When do you think is the right time? To get married, I mean."

"Well," Tweed says, "you either date someone and cheat on them for ten years and then marry them, or you marry someone young and cheat on them for the rest of your life. My advice: wait till you're done."

"That makes a lot of sense," I say. "It's practical."

"You forgot to shave today, Tyrone," Tweed says. "And when are you and me going to grab that steak?"

I know this is his sign-off so I answer, "Soon, I hope," which is mine.

O

I put on a few pounds and I lose a few pounds. I swim like a fiend so I can eat what I want and maintain an acceptable level of fatness. I don't have the genetics to take myself to the next level. The biggest lie is that swimming works every muscle in your body. I must work every muscle in my body. I watch Michael Phelps win medal after medal, President Bush cheers him on from the stands. I think about President Bush drinking a Benedictine & brandy with Michael Phelps, the former's favorite drink before he dried out. Of all the things the president fails to do, being an alcoholic is one of them.

I come from a long line of dippers. Sauce never talks back. Ranch sauce. Sugary ketchup. Chipotle sauce shows up, that's cool. I am the invisible man dipping chicken in sauce, running through Harlem sucking down yams, humiliated and finally happy. The watery chicken-finger sauce at Burger King, sides of Hoisin at Mr. Yip's, where I wolf down mounds of sugary chicken and a few pieces of gray-green broccoli. The chicken the size of Montana, the broccoli dots designating Montana's important cities.

I also have an alfredo problem.

Most of the people I work with also grew up in New York. I learn the names of out-there neighborhoods in Brooklyn like Sunset Park and I offer some Queens names as a return gift. We share what only people who grow up in New York care about. Like when a hurricane brews 3,000 miles away only people who live 3,000 miles away care about it. It's too bad for us that we're from this place, stuck in this place, that others move to in order to get unstuck. Secretly, we like it. You cannot stop New York City.

My eyes could be all of these things at the same time: glassy, kind, loving, focused, intense, peering, judging, sex-seeking and hiding in the squint of my smile. I want it both ways: not to be counted among the Indian-killing slave-owning part of White America but also to be even Whiter than that, to be Whiter and more wasteful of water than golf, to enslave the world, kill them all and be so American I don't even exist outside of my armored car, my Exxon-fueled throne, never an interregnum.

Yeah. I'm sitting in Mr. Yip's. No Muzak, no décor. In front of me piles of shrimp the size of Missouri, tails making the crooked borders, snow peas dotting the St. Louis metropolitan area. Mr. Yip's is cramped, minimal seating. Western-style Cantonese capitalism. I see it all, for some reason, if I look up from my plate. Hungry secretaries yell at the mouth-masked food line servers: "Get more chicken in that. Don't go being stingy."

In front of me crispy beef, arranged in the shape of California, the golden state's hundreds of irrigated golf courses the sesame seeds. No wonder I have golf anxiety. Tweed Spreckman wants to invite me on an outing with a minor COO at Goldman. The COO, a successful father of four, hardly ever leaves his silo. He wants to get out into green space and the mother nature of Northern New Jersey. Goldman Sachs is our #1 target. Goldman is the #1 target of every firm, especially Goldman itself. This is a priority relationship-building opportunity. Tweed doesn't ask me, "what's your handicap these days?" but that's what I hear because it's the only golf phrase I know. Well, what about bogey. Probably I should learn to play golf but the idea makes me sick. It stands for everything I am against. I imagine myself wearing a Titleist baseball cap, polarized sunglasses above the rim. I'm shining my hybrid throne, depositing debt-free children at top schools, we even own a purebred dog. I look up from my crispy beef and turn the angry *Post* to a semi-empty page—legal notices—and write down everything I know about golf. Tiger Woods plays golf. So does Jack Nicholson, but not the actor. Golf wastes water. The world's homeless population could live on American golf course land, if they wanted to move there. The game itself originated in Scotland, probably. But I need more. Golf metaphors, history. Golf skills. The jolly banker tosses off scripture—usually Saint James, no faith without the work of bankers—across the back nine to validate his takeovers. Where does this come from? Why am I here? In order to one day hear my voice echoing through the halls of American power, I will need to twist my hips.

My numbers foot, my reputation solidifies, but I suspect competency is a deterrent to advancement. I don't want to get too good at any one thing because it's all I'll be noticed for. A reputation needs to be a fluid. I must locate, in the steady corporate beat, a syncopation. This is something I should know how to do. I work long hours, tune-out the overhead TVs threatening Terror and Bloomberg, spit afterhours phlegm into my recycling wastebasket. I must avoid a reputation for sensitivity. The real rewards of bullets being consistent, the proper outcome of data in cells aligning flush right, the far-reaching goals of PowerPoint boxes lining up correctly is that one day I'll stop doing these things and have other people doing them for me, because they'll be younger and better at it than I am. The path to leadership is paved with forgetfulness. Management is distance. Keep far away what you want to do least. Keep even further away the most critical thing to get done. Bangalore is an ideal distance. Labor arbitrage is a young science. Retirement is not something that's *going to happen*. Retirement is happening right now. One day I will move somewhere really far away like Arizona and retire on a golf course. Instead of catching a connecting flight in Phoenix for a weekend in Vegas, PHX will be my home airport. I'll spend my golden years living in Mexican territory, a fake America state shaped like a breaded chicken cutlet. I'll steal water from working people to irrigate my golf course. My wife and I will become friends with another married couple and we will have a foursome. Maybe they'll also be from New York. We'll find out we went to the same high school, the same year, sat in the same homeroom but somehow we didn't know each other. I'll lower, or raise, my handicap, until I myself am handicapped. The only contact I'll have with Microsoft Office will be reinvesting its dividends in my portfolio. I'm going to do what's good for my bottom line. Put your reputation in your purse, I remember from *Othello*, put your reputation in your purse. But Iago was calculating, murderous, racist just to make himself popular, he was evil. I want to leave the office, where is this getting me, go loaf on the grass and read about sex in *The Farewell Symphony*. With that out of my system I take a deep dive into the other guy's system.

○

I team, brainstorm, I'm not even hungry but it's time to go to lunch. I've started leaving poetry and novels behind because switching gears from marketing to literature feels less and less possible. In fact, it is hard to imagine two professions which have less in common with each other. I was wrong about Frank O'Hara and me, we're actually quite different.

I ride the elevator down to the lobby and find myself out on Wall Street. I stand in front of the statue of George Washington at Federal Hall. The fingers on George's hand curl up like he's waiting to receive the ball back from his catcher. I start walking in circles, through the bordered federal district with street names like John and William, safe passage for the brainy and allegiant. The cobblestone alleys are a mirage of craftsmanship and every few steps there are topical detours, admittance restrictions. I distance myself from commentary, peddle past annoyances. Now I'm getting hungry. Sometimes I'm forced to slow down, zigzag my way forward like marbles moving through the silver edges of a child's maze. I walk forward, again and again, eyes in front of my feet. I don't lift my feet too high. I will not stroll. I must not take it all in. I notice less than ten percent of what's going on. I walk alongside workers who look like me, hometown heroes, lunch pail administrators, as Manhattan's extras we are box office stars. In their faces I see their parents, so proud the day their kids secured back office positions at the big banks on Wall Street. Some of us are not here, we work on the wrong side of the Hudson where the real money is exchanged, where the wayback-office operations of the city's set-piece capital clears. None of us are permitted to stand on the steps of the Exchange. Only cops, pigeons and the occasional squirrel make it through the metal barriers. The day's IPO banner waves like a flag in the wind. I see fearless tyrants, Dutch masters, outrage inspirers, hipless whores with mafia racks, spindly old men in New York Giants baseball caps who travel downtown to discuss market trends and fluctuations with their still-human stockbrokers. They're retired men with solid pensions and salad-fork manners who spend the cold months on Florida holiday. During the in-between months they have letters to post, nothing better to do. I see uniformed police officers and undercover police officers, orange cones. I see protestors, knocked-down cones. The protestors yell at me, the cops protect me. The protestors are bussed-in, rallying for an impossible state. They wear hooded sweatshirts and Halloween masks, hold up cardboard signs inked with magic slogans. Like everyone else in America, they want something from me. The police stop all of us so that a marching band can cross Broadway. Snare drums beat in the broken rhythms of war, piccolos sputter the basic hymns of the republic. What are they reenacting? Is it Veterans Day? The troop marches across Broadway, a narrow street this far downtown. I watch the puzzled expressions on everyone's face and make one myself in order to fit in. Sometimes, it's Christmas. Bulging wreathes in every lobby. It's a competition to see which bank can hang the biggest swinging wreath, pot the highest number of poinsettias. In the summertime, a homeless man steps to me near Washington's statue, a homeless man steps to me near the banks on Broadway, a homeless man steps to me in front of Alexander Hamilton's tombstone.

"You know, without him they'd be no *New York Post*."

"Thank God for him," I say.

He holds an empty cup and sheaves of loose leaf. I know this guy, I mean I know his character, pitching the same poem to everybody. His touch is feathery. The slimed feather of an oil suffering bird.

"I'm working on lunch here. Working on lunch. Poet of the pavement. Call me Pavement Poe."

Poe wears black pants with ripped knees, another layer of pants. His shower shoes have no tongues. I bet his homestead, before the hatred, had cats and rugs. There's this account over here, and that account, and the other account for later, the account for way later, and they are depleted one by one until there are no more accounts. When the accounts are gone, unseal the envelopes. There's a bunch of 20s in a manila envelope, with the return address of a company that fired you. Those 20s get spent. Then the coffee canisters. There's all this change saved up, that change is processed in a drugstore coin counter, a 9½ cent fee every dollar is assessed. The change is gone, solid objects disappear, and that's when perishables start to go. If the teeth grinded down during nights of bankrupt insomnia could be redistributed, those shavings would divine a mountain range of stress, bullying the Rockies, shadowing the Smokies. Poe is climbing this mountain, putting one foot in front of the other.

"Who's working on lunch? Pavement Poe. How close is he going to get to lunch?'

I find Poe annoying, but not as bad as the clipboard-carrying students saving soybeans and dolphins.

"You look like you shuffle papers," Poe says.

"That's exactly what I do."

"You know what Saint Matthew did? He threw *down* his papers and shuffled over to the Lord. What would you do if Jesus pointed at you?"

"I'd probably be like, who, me? This guy?"

"You know what Saint Matthew did?"

"Yeah, you told me."

"Of course I'm thinking of 'The Calling of Saint Matthew', the masterpiece by Michelangelo Merisi da Caravaggio, depicting the moment at which Jesus Christ inspires Matthew, the tax collector, to follow him. It was completed in 1600 for the Contarelli Chapel in the church of the French congregation, San Luigi dei Francesi in Rome, where it remains today."

A tourist hands me her camera. I move a few steps back, bend down, hold the camera up to my eye. I feel exposed without my natural vision. Through the lens I can see the family. They are trying not to smile, standing at the temporary ruins, but Poe and I know they want to.

"Come on, big smiles!" I say. "It's okay to smile, you're in New York City!"

They can't help it, they're on vacation, they must smile, especially when Poe says "sushi!"

Poe doesn't steal their camera. When they disappear into the crowd he gets back to his pitch. "Now you know my credo is to believe. My credo…you know credo means to believe," he explains, rustling his poetry papers, "…my credo is we should believe. Now listen to it right here. You see that? My credo? Believe."

"Got it. You gotta believe."

He raises his cup. I open my wallet. Gripping it tightly I remove two singles and drop them into Poe's cup. In my mind I see the shadowy outline of a future daughter, asking me to buy her Mister Softee.

"God bless you, brother," Poe says.

"What about a poem?" I ask, but he's already walking away and he disappears into the crowd.

I'm approached by a tourist from the American interior. Like every other man I see the first thing I notice are his shoes, white New Balance sneakers. He's wearing shorts, too, it must be summer, motherhood and apple pie. He is thin with a full head of white hair and small dark eyes. His face is a strange kind of white, curdled 2% milk, an interracial palm.

"I don't usually talk to strangers, but it's very spiritual down here," he says.

"Oh, yeah. It's the spiritual gift that keeps on giving. A holy annuity."

"Did you know this church was for 9/11 first responders."

"I did. I think we read the same *Time* article."

"Can I offer you a piece of advice? I saw you give that beggar your money. You know my wife and I went to Italy last summer."

"That's beautiful," I say. "Did you go to Rome?"

"We did."

"Did you see 'The Calling of Saint Matthew'? The masterpiece by Michelangelo Merisi da Caravaggio, depicting the moment at which Jesus Christ inspires Matthew, the tax collector, to follow him. It was completed in 1600 for the Contarelli Chapel in the church of the French congregation, San Luigi dei Francesi in Rome, where it remains today."

"We saw several masterpieces. The crowds were a mess. But we learned many things. We learned Michelangelo, the other one, didn't even wish to build the Sistine Chapel. It was work. It was a work order. You're not helping that man by giving him money, he's just going to buy drugs."

"Maybe he needs drugs," I say.

"Michelangelo didn't need drugs."

"Poe wasn't Michelangelo," I say. "He was homeless."

"Michelangelo was homeless."

"Really?"

"No," the man says. "I don't think so."

○

Breaking bread with other people is for communists. I prefer dining alone. I'm sick of Mr. Yip's and the line is too long at Burger King, eating pizza for lunch, I don't know, pizza's an in-between meal. I settle on the nearest food court in the basement of a midsized bank's global headquarters. The food court is muttering, sounds from the gallery before the judge approaches the bench, only the judge never appears in food court.

When I see the food choices I lose my appetite. I buy a coffee from a place called The Café of Celebration, which roasts turkey in natural juices. I take a seat, a sip, and the coffee burns my tongue. I go to Taco Bell, telling myself *I feel like Mexican today and I'm thinking outside of the bun*. I buy the bag, find a seat, turn the bag upside down and out drop the tacos, the hot sauce packets and enough napkins for a small family. I dig in, eat lunch like I mean it. I squirt sauce packets on cellophane, swipe tacos through sauce and spit out flecks of torn wrapper.

I chew and ask myself to name an industry unaffected in the short-term by how many it kills over the long-term. I realize those are all of them, pan-industry, all-county, all-state, all-world.

I find a pen and write down the list of people I've slept with on the front page of the *Post*. The list changes every day. What else is a young man supposed to do alone in a food court, if not bring his listing gaze to his conquests?

1) Mrs. Osorio
2) Professor Peter Gross
3) Martina in Little Park (taught me the phrase *hood rat*)
4) Another hood rat
5) Waiting, on a Sunday afternoon, for what I read between the lines
6) Hood rat
7) The grandmother from Pittsburgh
8) The chickenhead from Portchester
9) I'm not ready for this sort of thing
10) Hood rat

11) I would rather starve than eat your bread

12) Kiss, kiss, Jenny's lips (kiss, kiss, Jenny's, lips)

Part of me wants to ask Jenny to marry me. If only she would call me back, I would ask. I think she'd say yes.

"What have you been doing?" I ask when she picks up. "Why don't you call me back?"

"I'm sorry, Ty. I've slept with too many other guys to pretend anymore."

"You've got to stop going to Brooklyn."

"I know."

"At least I have the decency to only sleep with people from Manhattan."

"You're so human and decent, Mr. Meathead."

"It's okay. You're doing research."

"No, I'm horny."

"That's okay. It's natural at our age."

Jenny and I hang up without making a plan to see each other.

O

Banks, they say in focus groups, are the churches of Wall Street. I neither agree nor disagree with that statement. I search for the tray of holy water in the lobby entrance, step to the ATM and begin my transaction. I go into the bank when I have no business to transact and lean against deposit-slip furniture and flip through brochures about the benefits of applying for a home equity loan. In the quiet of the bank I hear my lunch-weighted breath, smell my own food making its way to my own stomach. I insert my card into the time machine, just to have something to do. The amount in checking is less than the amount on my credit card. Terms and agreements make this happen. It makes no sense to me but it makes sense to the lenders. Money is for counting. The direction makes no difference. That's how you know everyone is lying. Some men hear "things are tough for everyone" and they know that's not really the case. They hear "it's all relative" and they doubt that. They think things are going well, or at least moving along, and then they have a couple runs of bad luck and they start to think things were never going all that well in the first place.

Protesters are gathering on the corner of Pine Street and Broadway. They raise up American flag signs that read END DEPORTATION NOW!

An old black man wearing short chinos and an oversized hooded parka with giant silver snaps sucks in his teeth, says, "You'd think they'd be smarter than to advertise they're illegals."

What a chump. He doesn't realize *he's* illegal. I'm illegal too. We'll all be illegal in five seconds. Maybe we can go pick strawberries in California, slaughter cattle in Nebraska, snap chicken necks in Georgia.

"We'll all be illegal soon," I say matter-of-factly. He walks away, shaking his head at today's youth.

People and actual New Yorkers snap pictures of the immigration protestors. They bear the weight of being photographed. When I'm in the office, sitting high above these protestors, reading incisive, well-written articles about the impossibility of their success, I often picture an America where the businesses publishing well-written articles about protestors, exercising their mighty right to a free press, and the people taking pictures of protestors, exercising their mighty right to technology, are forced into a lifetime of hard labor. Their punishment? Joining protests. Or joining the cops. A world of protestors and cops, impervious to coverage. I think I've got the next war on my mind. That is my nifty idea, sitting high up above the proto-ruckus. Satisfied with my revolutionary vision I return my eyes to my screen and don't move a muscle.

A larger crowd of civilian photographers and a business-news photographer gather around the immigration protestors. Photographers now outnumber the protestors themselves. Outnumbering the combined number of protestors and photographers are dozens of heavily-armed cops who appear out of nowhere, like roaches when the lights turn on.

Me, I order an espresso. Or I say dollop of steamed milk. I order a biscotti with pistachios and ask for a plate. Nothing makes me happier than eating biscotti. It's basically just a fancy word for a twice-baked cookie. The best part of my adult life, what makes me realize I have the most freedom and I'm one of the luckiest people in the world, is that I can leave the office and go have a biscotti. An afternoon espresso and a biscotti on a saucer keeps you slim. Like celery, this is negative calories. For me, a biscotti is more than just a cookie. I bring my twice-baked cookie to the limited seating area near the hot food bar that goes half-price after 4PM. In front of me the condiment end cap. Heaps of individually-wrapped ketchups, relishes, spicy mustard, Dijon mustard, hot sauce, mayonnaise, cocktail sauce, sweet onions; individually-wrapped forks, knives, spoons; squirt bottles of creamy salad dressings and individually-wrapped packets of vinaigrette, olive oil, red vinegar, balsamic vinegar, pre-mixed oil and balsamic vinegar, six croutons with their Spanish-language nutrition facts. I see it all. My biscotti is gone before I know it. The sense of safety lasts for weeks.

The Future April

For charity itself fulfills the law,
And who can sever love from charity?
— Shakespeare, Love's Labour's Lost

My father grew up in the Bronx, moved to Queens after high school.
He went to Disneyland at 15, Las Vegas before he was 21. He's been
to the Grand Canyon, Virginia Beach, and he once stowed his last
Buick on a boat from the Delaware Water Gap to Cape May, New
Jersey. That is the summary of his travels. He played baseball in
high school until an injury took glory away. He dropped out of
college to trade on the floor of the stock exchange for much of his
life. I think of Dad when I see men downtown storming out of the
Exchange and lighting up Camel Full Flavors. He used to smoke and
he doesn't anymore, except sometimes. He used to wear the trader's
uniform, covered in decals of the banks who owned him. I call the
bank *who* because banks are people—banks are my Dad. But Dad
is no longer owned by a bank and that's a hard truth for a
businessman to accept. After he suffered a lower back injury,
unrelated to work, unrelated to anything I could ever understand,
he stopped smoking and started trading, with his own money, from
home. Then, my cousin, also a broker, invested in him, and Dad
never had to leave home again. He trades nothing fancy. He

forecasts, with a single-hitter's scrappy precision, the downturns and upticks of the major indices. He has a workingman's understanding of the art of speculation. My father doesn't look at the Dow and see the world's economic thrust, the energetic exchange of capital. Nor does he look at the Dow and see an ethical problem, the source of the world's unfairness and misery. What does Dad see when he looks at the Dow? Waking up early and going to work. The same steel the Buick builder sees when he builds the cars Dad no longer has the ability to drive.

My father should get out of Queens. He belongs in North Jersey or Florida like everyone else in our family, but he's stuck. He feels cooped up. Well, he rarely leaves the house. And if he does, he cries. Because the trees are so green. He's a great crier, my Dad. He cries at home too, when young men don't make it home from war. When women who resemble my mother are diagnosed with TV breast cancer. When he hears Randy Newman's theme music to *The Natural*, the sliding Brucknerian brass, the irritating Tchaikovskian flutes, the dusty timpani rolling as cleanup hitter Roy Hobbs limps to the plate, ignoring his bleeding guts, reordering his flow toward different guts. My father can't help it when confronted with baseball in its idealized form, and anyway he doesn't want to.

"That's what it's for, Ty. It's called a tearjerker for a reason."

At the foot of Dad's chair is a milk crate, overflowing with dead remotes, tangles of extension cords, outlet adapters and various plugs for appliances and electronics that no longer exist. On the folding table beside his recliner, on a dessert plate, a half-eaten Crab Rangoon. Next to his remotes, his most important possession, a large sippy cup filled with fruit-flavored Crush soda, usually pineapple, sometimes strawberry, or a tropical medley delivering six to eight percent of his daily vitamin C. He ingests and injects government-sponsored medication that accelerates his hair loss, reveals the light brown skullmark I long to kiss. He nibbles, slurps, savors, sleeps. In his milk crate he also keeps a spray bottle of no-streak glass cleaner, a roll of paper towels, a ripped undershirt wrapped around a can of lemon-scented Pledge, next to that a tall canister of bug spray, even though he's never seen a roach in the house. Neither have I. But I get the feeling Dad's waiting for it, that he's praying for vermin, to confirm his suffering, to know disgust is there in the form of a pest, to see disgust, to watch ugliness scamper across the rugs, a visible enemy which must be killed. My father makes me realize that if you don't give a businessman an enemy, he ends up attacking himself.

He turns the TV volume up. It's the middle of *Superman II.*

"Have you seen this?" he asks.

"Are you kidding?" I say. "I mean, are you serious?"

"Calm down. Of course I'm kidding."

Superman is confessing his love for Lois Lane to the apparition of his birth mother. She warns him that in order to turn out Lois, Superman must give up his superpowers, permanently. *If you want to love as a mortal, then you must live as a mortal.* Superman goes with it. "Mother, I love her," he says. And all for love, the superblood is drained from his body. He turns out Lois Lane in a silver beanbag chair. But when they return to the world, things go bad, fast. The real world is under attack and Superman is helpless to save it.

"Isn't that too bad for Superman," Dad says.

"The worst. I hate this part. I feel like no matter how many times I see it he's never going to get his powers back."

"Don't worry, he'll find the crystal," Dad says. He picks up his glass cleaner and paper towels and pushes himself almost off of his chair toward the TV screen. He starts wiping down the screen using circular motions, like it says to on the directions. He's wiping the blood off Clark Kent's face.

"Maybe you shouldn't clean the TV while it's on," I say. "Isn't that dangerous?"

"I don't think so. You know, Ty, I don't get these stations. They show *Rocky I, II, III, IV,* and *Superman I, II, III, IV,* and then they start all over with *Rocky.*"

"No overhead programming, I guess?"

"Have you seen *Rocky II?*" he asks me.

"Are you serious? What's wrong with you? I mean, have you lost it?"

O

Jenny Marks used to come over for dinner. We would have sex in my bedroom or shoot pool in the basement. The last time she came over she said she couldn't stay. We sat in the diner parking lot, got high and listened to *Kid A,* ate at the diner, and then back in the car we smoked again and listened to *The Bends,* eating the boiled chicken Jenny keeps in the backseat.

"She's too good to come in the house anymore?" my father asked when I came back alone.

One night the phone rings. It's Jenny.

"She must have nothing better to do," Dad says, handing me the phone.

"How are you doing?" I say into the receiver.

"It's Sunday," she answers. Her voice is low and sweet, tickling me like a finger on a part of my body I can't say where. Jenny says she can be right over. She says we can take a drive, if I'm not busy, what am I doing, how have I been, do I want to hang out. She sounds happy. Or maybe that's just me. I should yell at her, or hang up: she hasn't returned my calls or messages in weeks. But I say yes. And cancel, at the last minute, my after-dinner hookup with a hood rat. It occurs to me Jenny may be the biggest hood rat of them all, but I'm so excited, in love again with Jenny Marks, my Corona girl.

My father asks what she wanted.

"She wants to hang out. We're taking a drive."

"She only calls when it's convenient for her," he reasons.

"Well," I reason back, "when else are you supposed to call someone?"

I can't sit still in the living room. I wait on our stoop, use the hallway broom to brush away new snow. Finally, Jenny pulls up, gets out, and asks me to drive.

"How the hell could you see?" I say, using my gloved hands to brush snow off the driver's side windshield.

"You aren't busy, you're sure," she says, her words muddled, her voice cold.

"Stop asking me that. You know the answer."

She's wearing another man's black coat and her old Mets cap, ponytail through the adjustable back. There are bruises on her cheeks, scrapes on her palms. I'm staring at her, at her bruises, but she won't look at me.

"You've got to stop going to Brooklyn," I say.

"Just drive, Ty."

I throw out some suggestions but she doesn't even want to go to the diner.

"We could go back to school and sit in the circle. For old time's sake."

"Go to the airport," Jenny says. "Take Corona."

I drive slowly. Jenny says the name of a guy. I know who she's talking about. Not exactly. I remember his voice from Professor Gross' senior seminar, *The Autobiographical Fallacy*. Jenny and I made fun of his pretentious postmodern questions. The voice said ideas were transmittances, fallacies were true exchanges, the voice talked about anthropology without talking about colonialism, said the penis had been replaced by a pill, or any old dildo would do, said we're back to that idea again and a particular organic vulnerability may be lacking. He said the American family is a state of mind. He said the American family does not really exist. He also said there is no such thing as an American. Now I'm driving faster. This is my role. And now I am seeing his face clearly. A straight guy who manicured his eyebrows, leaned back in his chair and folded his hands above his chest. He once drank wine with me and my friends at the amphitheater. We mistrusted him. He was never one of us. I feel better knowing that! I ask Jenny what about him. Now I am seeing him better. He wore a custom belt buckle, leaned way, way back in his chair and tickled the inside of his ear with a pencil. An unclear, disputed man. A strike season champion. I ask Jenny why she sees him. Why she ever saw him at all. She tells me she thinks she's falling in love with him, even though she still loves me. She tells me to keep driving, the long-cut, Corona Avenue to LaGuardia. I drive ahead. I know my role.

"I want to get arrested," Jenny says.

"Should be easy to get arrested at the airport. Cops everywhere. Let's loiter in a 15 minute seating area for 16 minutes."

We park in short-term, a level coded by color. We aren't going to the airport to watch the planes take off, we aren't in search of departures. The spaciousness of the airport slows us down. In the terminal the hum of the airport mall and the regularity of announcements slows us down. This is a problem. Everything is a problem. We go to the travel supply store. We buy a neck pillow. We buy a travel speaker. We go to the café and buy a burnt coffee and lemon plastic danish and take it to the communal seating area. I place our travel products on the seat in front of us. I sip my coffee. Boy do I sip my coffee. Jenny watches a worker trim an artificial Christmas tree. I remind Jenny we are people with dreams. It's between you and your dreams, I say, but they are alive.

"You have to forgive me," she says.

"For what?"

"For everything."

"This is everything," I say, and I hate that I say it. I never say, what are you doing with me, why did you call me, why didn't you call a female for your female problems isn't that what all you females do in all your female movies.

"You shouldn't wait for me. I'm not the woman who waits for you, Ty."

"Come on," I laugh, crying now. "I know you're gone. I know it's over between us. You are good. You don't set your alarm on weekends. And we love wine."

"Dionysus," she says.

A gentleman, I remember, is someone who can play the accordion, but doesn't.

"Dionysus. And the birth of Dionysus, you know, it's a mystery. No one knows where he came from and he always came late. Homer was scared of him. Because he was anti-war. It can't be footnoted, wine. Tonight will be swept under. A footnote. This is not your text."

Jenny gives me the neck pillow. She gives me the travel speaker. I never use them on planes. We go back to the car. I drive her car home. I tell her to take some NyQuil and she says, no, remember, it keeps me up. Oh yeah. I walk back to Dad's and think about what I've just done. I feel a bit like a cheat and liar telling Jenny she will forget tonight, that this is not her text, because I will never forget tonight, not tonight, not tomorrow, and this is the only text I have. I want only romance, moonlight, empty lifeguard chairs until you and I get there, all my seasides, all my stars. But often I embrace women running away from teething men. Shivering women ending up in my arms. Let's wait for the bus, I have a pass. Drive me somewhere, I have a car. The drive uptown and the drive downtown. The drive to the West Side highway and the drive through the park, the park drive back east. The drive down Grand Avenue in Queens turning into Flushing Avenue in Brooklyn. The drive down Corona Avenue or the drive down the FDR and over the Triborough to LaGuardia for a last-minute flight no one could afford, for a flight not cancelled or delayed, a flight never even booked, no uncomfortable seat in our future. I learn too many things I don't want to learn because knowledge isn't a separatist. I cover women in blankets and smother them with platitudes as we sit forever in parked cars or we drive on the treacherous boulevards, McGuinness in Brooklyn, Queens in Queens in our tricked-out Toyota, cherry-red BMW 328i, grandpa-green Volvo 244GL, snowy black Jetta, colorless Ford sedan, no blankets, some blankets, coolers, no coolers, shouldering platitudes at the worst hour of gray midmorning sunlight, sitting in a parked car until making up our minds to drive somewhere lonelier than a parked car. Drive the car,

remove the blankets, talk about weather, fry one egg, one piece of
toast.

Sepia-toned tributes to female violence, fuck 'em. Numbness,
like pain, comes in degrees. But there's no hurt when I get back to
Dad's house, only bothersome twitching. I think about Jenny's
man, the man I am seeing clearly, the man who knew the American
family does not exist, the man who hated western-style capitalism,
but I am not a man who hunts other men. Besides, he lives in
Williamsburg, I see his rooftop clearly now, I was there at a party,
he lives with three guys I actually might like, and I'm not
schlepping to Brooklyn. And he's not the only man left. There will
always be more and more men erasing men from my memory.

○

My father sits in his recliner, watching *Rocky III*.

"What happened?" he asks.

"Nothing."

"I told you, only when it's convenient for her."

"It's not that. It was convenient for me, too. Sorry," I say,
laughing until I cry. "I don't understand how to love someone."

"If you don't have love," Dad says, "you don't have any power.
It's a great power and it understands for you."

"The resounding gong," I say, and I hate to realize it, because
it is my father, and because it is love, but I don't agree.

"You can't force it," Dad says.

My whole life he's been telling me not to force it. Don't force
a three-prong plug into a two-prong socket. Don't force the table
leaf into the table base. And his advice on my earliest sexual

encounters, variations on the theme of not sticking it in. Don't force it. See what fits. See what it's willing to give.

"I have to force it," I say. "I don't have a choice."

○

When I don't know what to do, I do laundry. I lug the hamper down to the basement and color-separate Dad's sweats, towels, bathrobe, underwear, knockaround polos, pleated green chinos. I shoot bumper pool during the spin cycle, bump the butt of my cue into pipes and Mom's storage boxes, or I do nothing but listen to the laundry soak while I consider Martha and Mary from Luke's gospel. Jesus makes a pit stop in the house of these two women. Mary bows, pays tribute to the Lord. Martha, though, keeps at her chores. Jesus warns Martha to calm down, chill out, be more like Mary. *Martha, Martha, you are worried about too many things.* I am like Martha. Dad is like Mary. He is concerned with just *one* thing (the blue-chip stock, the pizza in front of him, the playoff game) and I am concerned with too many things.

I run down to the basement, I run back up.

Permanent Press takes on a double meaning.

I wash and wash Dad's clothes, and soon enough, he mocks me, I'm just washing the machine. But what is a man to do, if not laundry? The flavorful scent of high heat steam reminds me of baby's first Christmas, and the towels harm no one when they're fluffy and soft. I press Shout on his heaviest marinara stains, prewash in the basement sink. I help him get into his everyday sweats, Smart Buys at the drugstore. To church, the better set, from the sporting goods store, pima cotton. And his thuglife Champion hoodie, *Champion* spelled out at the old-school breast, hood up on his bald scalp, pale as a gunned-down rapper. I sniff the glowing towels, sway to the music of the next load, hear the man's voice in a seminar auditorium. I am hearing him clearly now. Boy I am seeing this dude.

The smell of a warm towel is the smell of incest. The smell of a warm towel is the smell of incest. The smell of a warm towel is the smell of incest.

We have fewer and fewer towels. Why? Where do they go? Are we turning each other out? What are we doing to them? There used to be towels and towels and towels and towels, now there are just towels and towels and towels.

I whistle while I wash, a towel work song.

Towels and towels and blankets and blankets and hampers and towels and towels and towels. Towels and dishcloths and towels and towels bookcases towels and towels and towels. Cues and towels, sheets, towels, napkins, sheets, napkins, towels—towels and towels, towels and towels, towels and towels and towels and towels.

O

I meet our upstairs boarder on the basement stairs. Maybe he's stealing our towels. He lives on the third floor of our house, an illegal space with windows looking into rooms but no windows to the outside. This attic is where my grandfather lived before he died. Then came the boarder. Actually, we've had about twenty upstairs boarders and they all disappear for various reasons at various levels of having paid rent.

Juan is an aggressive death-metal guitarist. One of the nicest guys you'll ever meet. He helps my father with things around the house that need complicated fixing. When I run into Juan on the staircase landing, my hamper is full of just-folded towels and the good napkins we never use.

"Day's work is never done," Juan says in a deep voice, slight pride in his idiom, long silvery-black hair falling over his eyes. We both smile. His teeth are stained brown, his boots and jeans black, heavy keychain on the belt clip. He wears a black denim jacket sewn with metal band patches.

"I heard you're good at pool," he says. "We should play."

"The table is like half the size of a bar table."

"How's your Dad's health," he asks.

"Fine," I say, cutting myself off. Dad's health is none of Juan's business.

What I know about Juan I learn from Dad and some research. He works as an apparel salesmen at a Herald Square discount store where everything must go because it is under new management. Late into the night Juan composes music, supports the metal community. He subs in bands that pound out buck-a-head gigs in the bars along 37th Avenue in Jackson Heights. He knows death. Now more than ever. He knows professional wrestlers. He used to play guitar in a band whose Nordic name I can't pronounce. They were once described on a no-longer-updated website as the crippled love child of Richard Wagner Nixon and a re-wombed Goneril Lear.

Juan's a sweet loner, a reliable session guy. One band won't tie him down. According to my father he's a happy Satanist, one of the hundreds of hard-working avant-garde composers living in the illegal attics of Queens. Men dedicated to their music, survivors of unbelievable sorrows, realistic about extreme metal fame and slightly decreased unknowingness. To become less unknown, in fact, would probably be a kind of failure.

Jenny isn't calling me back. Dad's half-asleep in his recliner, I'm squeezing my balls on the couch. The playoff game is over and we're watching *Superman II*. I'm fighting off sleep to watch the opening sequence of *Superman III*.

"You want a pill?" Dad asks.

"Maybe. What is it?"

"It's green. They're strong. Take only half. Nibble it."

I swallow the whole pill. After the opening credits of *Superman III* I must leave the couch and go to my bedroom.

I go to bed. Then I get out of bed, find a broom, sweep the floor. No matter how many times I sweep it's still dusty. I sweep again. I'm wide awake. Maybe Dad's green pill is having an opposite effect on me, like NyQuil does for Jenny. I blame my tossing and turning on bad luck, the night bird, and then I hear music coming from upstairs.

Music of rip-roaring insanity.

Juan is composing death metal music, aggressive and hyper-technical, punishing, blackened, seersucker-rending sludge.

I can't make out the lyrics.

Short growls.

Rabid grunts.

Maelstroms of fiery wit.

America has ended, please bring your refuse to the front of the theater.

Now I can make out the lyrics. The coarse topics are total death, population annihilation, a fallen Christ, a risen Devil, the morbid events of the crucifixion retold boastfully and with ecstatic glee. No redemption. No hero-in-training. No transpersonal figure rising from the ashes: only whiteness, desolation, bleakness, the opposite of procreation and the reverberating madness of anti-ambrosial gut-scraping mayhem. Some of the lyrics in the half-tempo B section of the third movement, right before a blistering instrumental, call for the clitoral destruction of Mary, and for the mutilated organs of unholy sinners to be shoved in her pretentious pussy, followed by the dismemberment and cannibalization of the Holy Twelve as Mary watches from a rat-infested coven or dungeon.

I am freaking out.

Why didn't we lease the attic to a folk singer?

It occurs to me that Juan *is* a kind of folk singer, that this man, blaspheming what I hold dear, may be on the right track. I long to find out, make friends with him. I should get out of bed, float upstairs on the cloud of Dad's green pill and knock on Juan's door. Hey, now's as good a time as any for that game of pool. We will shred the morning and Mary will still be suffering. I'll tell him my thoughts on Jusepe de Ribera's *Saint Mary Magdalene in the Desert* and how this picture leaves me starved, like Joe Gillis in *Sunset Boulevard,* for a white shoulder. Juan will yawn. And I will blush, tell him disregard my crockpot allusions, it's Dad's green pill talking, not me.

Instead I toss and turn, alone, stuff my pillow between my legs like it used to work when I had growing pains as a kid. I can see now that I was foolish to curse my childhood before bedtime. My elbows weigh a ton. Again, I should act. I should get out of bed and go upstairs and thank Juan for helping my father remove the AC units from the windows. Instead I hum the cat-feet piano intro of Paul Simon's "One Man's Ceiling is Another Man's Floor." I hum for like five hours. Morning breaks, Mary is still suffering, and I promise myself I'll never ingest the green pill again.

I go to the living room. My father is asleep in his recliner. The muted TV is once again showing *Superman II*. While we were sleeping or while we were awake the station played Superman *III*, *IV*, *Superman: The Movie*, and now it's back to *II*, playing a scene I know very, very well.

Once again, Superman is horny. He needs to clear it first with his Mom. He activates the crystal that prompts her appearance. She is a vision. She takes her evanescence seriously. She stands tall, poised in the afterlife, her elegant gown adorned with zirconium ornaments. Midway through her words she offers the confused Superman her erotic exhortation. I mouth it to myself, through the muted TV.

If you want to love as a mortal, then you must live as a mortal.

Dad stirs, presses the volume up on the remote. "Isn't that too bad for Superman," he says groggily.

How my father loves his pain. *Nibble it*, he told me, regarding his knockout medication that sent my heart racing.

"Let me ask you a question. How do you plan on sleeping through Juan's music? Actually, let me first ask you this question: does Juan's music exist?"

"I don't hear it, really."

"You don't hear it? So it doesn't exist."

"Of course it exists. He's very dedicated. It doesn't bother me. I'm a heavy sleeper, you know that."

"What's he paying?"

"Fifteen more than the last guy."

"Who never paid it. You should raise his rent," I say, lowering my voice. "You should raise the rent on a death metal composer who works in the early hours. No other renter in America has this kind of amenity."

"He's already paying a fortune."

"If by 'fortune' you mean 'market rate.'"

I want to run out of the house, never return, but all I do is return. I don't acknowledge Dad's otherworldliness, except as a benchmark for my own problems. *Well, at least I'm not as messed up as he is.*

"Your mother's memorial service is coming up."

"In three weeks."

"That'll be here before you know it."

O

Dad's ready to go. He's wearing his one suit, doorman fit, his last few hairs styled with brilliantine, combed to make pickets. He's wearing salt-damaged brown loafers and dark sunglasses so the world can't talk back. Who knows what the question might be? He has two ties left, one with NBA logos, one with NHL. He wants to wear the NHL, even though it's one of those three days of the year when it isn't hockey season. He asks me what I think and I tell him whatever he thinks, there's plenty of offseason activity in all sports so all sports ties are always in style. He agrees, but picks the NBA anyway, and needs my help making the knot.

We leave the house and walk down the hill. Dad allows himself deep breaths. He remembers how wonderful it is to be outside, walking in the sunlit air. What a big day this is for him. He feels young again, tells me the story. My mother and his sister, my Aunt Charlene, who now lives in Northern New Jersey, and did not come back to Queens for my mother's service today, they both worked, back in the day, at the same Five and Ten in Times Square. There isn't much more to the story. Dad went into the Five and Ten for a pack of gum. Eyes met. He asked her out. People went on serious dates back then. I elaborate from TV memory, envision lunch counters and meticulously designed set pieces, pocket squares and mended garments. Sinatra not at first recognizable as Frank, maybe it's only Julius La Rosa.

"We were young," my father says, "We had time. I feel young today."

He has difficulty scaling a short curb. I lift him on a three count and we cross the boulevard and rest for a few seconds against a bench a block away from church, so Dad can continue feeling young again.

"Who's to say what makes people happy," he says. "You can't force your feelings."

Our church, one of the first in America, colonial remod, struggles to recruit new members. Broke as a ghetto doorbell, one structural deficiency away from ruin, it rents monthly parking in order to pay utility bills, uses a letterboard to spell inspirational slogans, from Ellen to Plato, below the Eucharist and confession times. We enter through the bank-like front door, dip two fingers in fecal matter holy water. Seating is cramped but the aisle is wide, to accommodate brides and pallbearers. The stations of the cross line the walls, advertisements for the powers of Roman pigs. At the altar there are glowing rows of candles, for meddling in the lives of the sick and dead.

We take seats in the back, our view partially obstructed by a beam. I see the nuns my mother adored, her final beautician, the diner counter waitress who poured her coffee, dressed for a shift she either just left or is going to after mass, and I see three of my so-called aunts, third-removed women on my mother's mother's side, infants found on doorsteps between the World Wars. They know secret stories but they never get around to telling them. I know them as shrinking ladies, baking what serves eight to twelve, women of the bobby socks, black and white moralists with poor circulation and rose-colored perms.

A church service is a short film: once it begins you wonder if it will ever end. The second reading recounts Saint Peter's escape from prison. Near the end of the story King Herod, Peter's jailor, orders the prison guards executed. They failed to meet expectations. It makes me suddenly happy to think of cops being executed, but then I feel bad.

"Your crimes are horrible," the future pope tells breaking-down Michael Corleone, "and it is just that you suffer."

What are my crimes? Is it just that I suffer, even if I do?

Upon hearing the call for communion, I help my father into the queue. The Nigerian priest raises the chalice. The choir doesn't sing. Other than the footfalls of the assembling flock and the weakening of the nails supporting the stations of the cross the only sound in the house of worship is the meandering music of the keyboard organ patch. On the line in front of us, I'm shocked to see our boarder, Juan. What the hell is this Satanist doing in church? I recall my green-pill induced sleepless night, the darkening hell, the smoldering buffoonery. When we return to our seats I mention Juan to my father, who, because of his inability to genuflect, is sitting way forward on his seat, face immobile behind dark glasses.

"What do you think of that?" I ask.

Dad delivers his second oldest joke: "the communion wafer could've used a little salt."

"How do you get to Carnegie Hall?" I whisper as a prayer. "But aren't you a little surprised? I'm not saying I'm surprised. A little, maybe."

"No," Dad says. "Juan is very passionate."

"Have you seen him here before?"

"I only come with you."

The silent prayer is an easy time to feel religious, but I don't close my eyes. I see nothing but Juan. Every face is two-faced, but this man composes music about the dismemberment of holy men, the desecration of holy land. There are putrefying hands, I recall, shoving themselves places putrefying hands don't belong.

It's time for the roll call of the sick and the dead. I hear Mom's name on the side of the dead. Dad and I close our eyes. When we open them, our aunts are looking back at us with sentimental faces.

Now the mass is over and even God is dead.

One of my aunts says hello, kisses me on both cheeks. Her breath smells horrible, a totality of radish. She informs me she heard I'm carrying on in Manhattan. She offers to walk my father home. Dad thinks it's a good idea. I can go to the Little Store, reup his soda and cold cuts.

I say goodbye, run as fast as I can out of church.

O

I feel out of place in my own neighborhood, snobbier and more removed than ever. I see the storekeepers and streetsitters whom I count among my strangest friends, and my favorite houses, they are also old friends, scarlet houses with overgrown gardens, vandalized gazebos and landmark plaques, red brick apartment buildings with window-unit ACs elevated on wooden blocks, upper-crust names like The Oregonian and The Van Loon Apartments. I see the reddest-faced men from church going to the subway saloon for their first shot and beer since before church began, and immigrant mothers pushing naturalized children across Justice Avenue. When I see young mothers I cry for my mother. A cascade of cherished allusions tumbles down my mind.

She once told me that the three prettiest words in the English language are *fresh cut flowers*.

I remember that.

I hum "I'll Remember April"—the shared month of our births. The lyric promises—*remember April and you'll be glad*. I think about how we'll be together again, in the future April.

Then I think about and start humming Wayne Shorter's song "Iris."

In order to cut this shit out I need to transact money.

I enter the Little Store and buy Dad's cold cuts and Crush soda. I consider the Diet Crush option, but that's not what he'll drink. I've tried before to put a few spoons of sugar in the diet, two packets of Equal, but for whatever reason that doesn't work and he knows it. "There's a reason they sugar it in the factory," he says.

Next, I go to the flower shop where it's cold and damp, the coolers humming. The bearded florist wears socks and sandals, has a cigar in his mouth.

"How's business?" I ask.

He chews his cigar, grunts. A ripped poster on a cooler reads: *Flowers are the earth laughing.*

"I'd like some fresh cut flowers. Irises. Are they in season?"

"Everything's in season," he says.

"Cool. Make them look expensive."

He trims the stems, adds the ruscus filler and two packets of plant food, closes it up with his big stapler. He ties colored ribbons around that and secures the arrangement in a cone of heavy plastic. I have mixed feelings. A lot of waste goes into floral arrangements.

The florist hands me a blank card and I push my handwriting to fill it with good words.

Mom: Remember April—you'll be glad.

I don't even recognize my own handwriting. The top of the card says: *Happy Veterans Day*.

I hear Mom laughing at me.

Whenever we graze, her and I, what dopes we are, the ditziest sheep in the flock.

I walk down the hill.

I see Juan in front of me, carrying a forty in a brown paper bag. He's so close I can hear his heavy-metal belt-loop keychain jangling.

I hang back, follow Juan at a medium distance. He turns into Little Park, a semi-restricted area between two apartment buildings. My childhood park. Home to the graves of my imaginary friends. There had been Amelia, an airline pilot, and Johannes, sometimes a composer, sometimes an astronomer. I was such a literal little boy that even my imaginary friends were historic personalities.

Little Park is a shithole. It has the profound will of a park, the forms and shapes of a park, but it cannot execute on them. The slide has no slide, the see-saw no board, no city leaf on the gate or rules for curbing dogs. And no chance of curbing the human exchange, either. The benches, with loose slats or missing them entirely, are set back far from the sidewalk, covered by overgrown bushes and sickly trees.

I crouch down behind these bushes in order to observe Juan. He sits on the darkest bench, retrieves a soft pack of generic full-flavor 100s from the inner pocket of his denim jacket. After lighting the cigarette he screws the cap off the 40oz and takes a big swig. I feel like I can taste his beer in my own mouth, that first sip of beer on Sunday after church, the day's first real event.

I get off my knees, walk over to his bench and introduce myself. Exhaling smoke, Juan laughs and says he knows who I am.

"That's right," I say. "We still need to play pool."

He offers me a cigarette. I sit down, place my mother's irises and my father's cold cuts and Crush at my feet.

We smoke in silence.

Juan has a lot of black hair, tied in a ponytail. He wears a white button-down shirt over his usual black t-shirt. When he looks at me to answer my first question—"how are you doing today?"—his dark-skinned face shines with vampiric paleness. His left eye droops and seems to lean at too great a distance away from his other eye, narrower than the good eye and reddened into a hideous rash, like a permanent blister boils under the lid. I sense that Juan is ugly, and embarrassed to engage in the simple act of looking, in the never-ending commitment and duty to open your eyes.

"Pretty good," he says. "How are you, Ty?"

"Great, Juan. Saw you at Mass."

"Saw you too."

He passes the 40oz and I take a big sip. Then I take another one, ramble on about his metal music. "How is your career going?" I ask. Flattery is the easy way to avoid making a real connection. When I meet someone famous, or meet someone that I believe to be a star in my personal constellation, I let them know *I just love their work*. What exactly am I saying to them? That I really love myself, cannibal-like, that I love my own *taste*. And I tell Juan his music is so interesting. All the progressive movements in metal these days! Everything splintered-off, wrapped in deluxe packaging. The internet, too, an exhumed grave of decaying information, like Linear B, a bunch of to-do lists and inventories, a death knell to the problem of multi-channel distribution.

"What's Linear B?" he asks.

"An ancient scroll. I think. Saw a special on it."

Juan doesn't say much in response. We both sense I'm nervous and talking out of my ass. He retrieves a blunt from his jacket pocket, lights it and takes two puffs, coughing forcefully with a wet sound, similar to how a dying person coughs only without ethereal sniffling. "Who are the roses for," he asks, blowfishing his cheeks.

"No one. Me, I guess. They're irises, actually. We didn't even go to the cemetery today. I should just leave them here. They're probably the only flowers that've been in Little Park all year."

"Little Park?"

"That's what we called this place when I was a kid. The Little Park. The Little Store. You know how little everything is in this hood. Except Hoffman Park. We used to call that Big Park. Where the basketball courts are."

"It's amazing you grew up here," Juan says, passing me the blunt. "Sorry about your mother."

"Thanks," I say, taking a courtesy hit. "How'd you know?"

"Your Dad. And the *Tablet.*"

"You read the *Tablet* too, huh."

"Word for word."

"Not just for the Wendy's coupons."

"For those too."

I tell Juan that the Wendy's in question turned into a McDowell's for the filming of *Coming to America*, and we share a joke about Queens being filled with a lot of common places, but what I'm really thinking about during this part of our conversation is community and belonging: if Juan clips the same Wendy's coupons that I do out of our church newsletter, that means we are a member of the same community, dipping fries in the same Frosties. That means, maybe, that Juan is my friend.

"Your Dad said you gave up your music scholarship?"

"Scholarship. Parents love that word, you know. Scholarship. Honor roll."

"Yeah man but there must've been a lot of people who applied. I don't even read music!"

"That doesn't matter. Believe me you care more about your music than I do. My Dad thinks you're very passionate."

We regard each other without saying anything, our mouths obscured by smoke and beer. Juan lets his hair out of the ponytail. I think of the phrase "soft to the touch" without knowing what it means. His face is ugly. His hair is beautiful, smooth, untangled. Avoiding his scary left eye, I watch his healthy right eye. It is small, dark, inward-looking. Only then do I realize that Juan is at least a generation older than me.

We sit in silence. He passes me the blunt again and I smoke more than I should. Cannabinoids encourage the brain stem of adolescence and I don't need any help.

"I had sex for the first time in this park," I finally say.

"Nice. Big dick, little park."

"Yeah, that's right."

"Who was the lucky lady?"

"This girl. Martina. She moved to Florida the next day."

"Because you banged her so hard."

"Probably. She is probably not the first girl to lose her virginity in Little Park and then be forced to move to Orlando. I remember getting the condom on more than I remember anything else."

"Was there blood?"

"No blood. And we'd been promised blood. That's the whole point of sex, right, the blood. It's weird. It's not the first time I saw a pussy, or touched one, but it was the first outdoor pussy I saw, and the first time I realized it smells. You think the smell gets in the air outside quicker than it does inside?"

Juan takes three short hits on the disappearing blunt and says, "That's why original humans probably moved sex into caves."

"But for hundreds of thousands of years they had sex outside. Like six-hundred-thousand years. You know, actually, that wasn't even my first time. My music teacher molested me, I guess."

"Yeah?"

"Yeah. I never told anyone that. But I mean look at me, I'm not like breaking up about it. I wanted it so bad, so is the word for that still molest?"

"No. Pardon my French, but that's called screwing," Juan says, flicking the blunt stub away. The fingernails on his fingerpicking hand are long, filing-board shaped. He wears a ring on every finger: a spider, a black lizard, a light silver stone, a dark silver stone, a black onyx, and one that doesn't seem to belong, on the left ring finger, a square stone the color of licked butterscotch. I think to myself that this ring means something more than jewelry, that he wears it not for him, but for somebody else.

We take big sips on the 40oz. I taste something like spilled beer, or beer saved from a spill when you're drunk, beer that when sober you'd wipe away, not drink. I've had so much beer I'm at the point I need more. I listen for a sound from the park's nature, a sour bird in the dying tree or more likely a rat scurrying across the cracked concrete, a disturbed pigeon pecking at a wall. I hear nothing. I smell Martina, like a candy ring.

Finally, I ask Juan my nagging question. It's none of my business, but why does he go to church on Sunday if he writes such blasphemous music, denouncing the very God whose body he accepts?

"For the Wendy's coupons," he says. But then he says naturally, as if he's been asked the question before, maybe by people who are making fun of him, that he doesn't think of it in black and white terms. Or maybe that's it—there is only black and white. He doesn't believe in gray. He doesn't believe in gray! He is praising the same things, glorifying the same heights, as our cheerful Nigerian priest. He's just doing it from the other side of the father.

"My music doesn't bring me any peace," he says. "I wait for it. It doesn't happen."

"That's cool. I mean, that's amazing. No peace. I couldn't wait. That was my problem."

"Word. I wait and wait, but there's no peace. No peace, nope."

"You don't get any peace."

"None, man."

"Do you want to walk?" I ask. "Especially at work," I go on, "I don't get any peace. My boss, or I guess I'm supposed to call him my manager, is making me hire people now. I have to look in someone else's eyes and listen to them tell me how they don't want to be free anymore, that they want to make money, that what they value is teamwork, and collaboration, instead of sitting in a room all day by themselves, alone."

"Some people do get peace from that nonsense."

"We just hired this girl. The new girl. I can't stop thinking about her."

"Nice. But don't let that distract you too much from your business."

"Yeah. What do you think, you want to walk?"

Juan shakes his head, takes another blunt out of his pocket, says he'll linger.

"It's like the Schubert G major. It's in a major key, sort of, but it's not happy."

"No peace, Ty."

"Yeah there's no serenity in that shit. Only the broken military march. Men march to the drums of war, only the men are broken and the animal skins of the drums are ripped. The soldiers are dead. Their orders carried out. The prisoners are dead. The prison guards are dead. The men are dead and the women are dead and the children are dead. The nations have failed. Only the war survives. And now, we have peace."

"No peace," Juan says. "She hates us all."

I pick up Dad's cold cuts and Crush, Mom's flowers. I remove the card and offer Juan the irises. "Or leave them here. It'll make this shithole look better."

He accepts the flowers, smiles and nods, like he suddenly has no idea who I am.

"You're right," I laugh. "She hates us all, Juan, doesn't she."

"She does. She hates us all."

O

Dad is asleep in his chair. I have to lean in close when he sleeps this hard, make sure he's still breathing.

What if he dies?

I want to know the exact minute.

He stirs when the volume suddenly increases during the commercials. The movie is *Rocky IV.* It is up to one of the quietest scenes. Rocky and his support crew arrive in Russia to begin this movie's grueling training sequence. It is the end of the first day, and Rocky is up in his bedroom loft nudging pictures of inspirational figures into the edges of his mirror. His new trainer, Tony, comes upstairs to give Rocky a pep talk. Tony tells Rocky about his deep feelings for Apollo Creed, who died earlier in the film, and whom Tony used to train. He says: *When he died, a part of me died.*

"Isn't that too bad for Tony," Dad says.

I hate my father at that moment. It's his big line, what makes him feel superior. Isn't-that-too-bad-for so-and-so on TV. Another year, another month, another week, another Sunday at church to learn something new about himself, to improve himself starting right now, and all he did was go back to the chair, still wearing his NBA tie, ready to nibble his next green pill.

His stationary qualities. His voice my nervous breakdown. His emotions my hysterical commitment. Buried in my 44-inch chest, never to be spoken, what he locked away in his heart the day he met me.

"Do you have to judge me on this day?"

"What do you mean? I didn't say anything."

"Do you have to judge me on your mother's memorial day?"

"I'm not judging you. We didn't even go to the cemetery."

"I can hear you talking in your brain," he says.

He's such an asshole.

He knows that's my worst fear, that he can read my mind.

I hate him even more.

You didn't hear me say that.

I leave the couch and return to my room. I locate a vinyl recording of the Schubert G-major piano sonata. I write a note to Juan, using my dark gray stationery with the light gray trim.

Dear Juan,

This is what I was talking about. Check it out. I hope this brings you no peace. She hates us all, doesn't she. She really hates us all.

Yours,

Ty

Later that night I can't sleep. An image, incessant, Mom's last meal. It's one of the oldest memories I keep, but it always takes place in the future, three moons out the hospice window, long-term cosmic care space station. What I see are the utensils of the future. Postconsumer spork. Postconsumer tray. Levitating salt and pepper shakers that move from hospice room to hospice room, the grand compromise of 2046, the socialization of elder facility condiments. The food, though, is old-fashioned, earth-bound. A traditional dead woman's feast. Grilled mashed chicken breast, French-cut mashed green beans, glazed julienne carrots smashed down into a puddle of chunky beta carotene. No wonder Mom hasn't eaten in a full 24 hours. When I get to the hospital after school, it's going on 36.

"She isn't hungry today," Dad says to me.

I nod, like I know what that means. Like he could possibly know what that means. But my father is never stronger, younger, braver, than when he leads Mom to death. He is filled with a vigor that perhaps he doesn't recall, one that only I remember and I must remember it vigorously. This man, this great crier, he didn't, in front of me at least, cry then. He brought clarity and solitude to every aspect of the end of my mother's life, even sang her Zeppelin's "Thank You" and found a way not to be a crier about it, no "tears of love lost in the days gone by," as Robert Plant presumed, at least none rolling down Dad's cheeks whenever I too was in Mom's room.

Here was the saddest thing right in front of him, death of wife, death of mother, but he got through it better than he could get through watching Roy Hobbs hit his home run in *The Natural*. Like everything else in our family we even mourned backwards, wept like squatters. Greeting cards send us into conniption fits, but if you promise to die long, slow, and horrible, and offer your sick body to medicine the way you offer your healthy body to the Lord, we will help you stay strong, we will stay strong, and help you get it all over with.

"She said your name," Dad says with a look of disgust. "Don't be fearful."

"I am not fearful," I say bravely. "I will get her to eat."

I am small and just making it up to the food tray. I scoop up some mashed chicken breast and hold the spork to her mouth. She won't budge or move her lips, which are dry, pale, their living redness gone.

"I don't need food, Tyrone."

"Call me Ty. Maybe you'll be hungry later," I say.

"I don't think so, honey."

"I'll wrap up the leftovers."

"No, take it away."

"You've got it eat."

"No. Just take the food away. Take the food away and you come here."

We hug until she closes her eyes. Then I raise the spork up to my own mouth. Turns out mashed chicken breast tastes pretty good. I eat all of her mashed chicken breast and I eat her salty carrots.

I wake up, get out of bed, find the broom and sweep the floor. Then I find my mother's favorite poetry book, a hardcover edition of William Carlos William's poems, introduced and selected by Randall Jarrell. I find the poem "Waiting", which she bookmarked with a dried flower. Mom knew how to wait. My father knows how to wait. Jenny knows how to wait, and she certainly keeps me waiting. My boss, Tweed Spreckman, he's impatient and racist and cruel, but he also, in a sense, knows how to wait, at least he knows how to wait for me to do his dirty work. Pavement Poe knows how to wait. Juan knows how to wait. But me, I don't know how. I can't even wait to read the poem called "Waiting" and those clipped, final lines that don't really fit with the rest of the poem.

What did I plan to say to her
When it should happen to me
As it has happened now?

In the middle of the night a vision of my mother comes to me. We are in a blue version of her final room. Her breasts are back. She sits cross-legged on the bubbling floor, overcome with grief. She is covered in shit, the shit that drips from the walls in dreams. But this is a room to treasure, where promises can be made. She is surrounded by the greatest art books in the world, the complete drawings and paintings of major and minor masters, modern painters and classical painters, books with trilingual perspectives penned by multilingual essayists and fold-out color plates on bonded paper. These are the products she adored and she sits in the middle of them and in the middle of them is shit. And the waitress from the diner, who poured my mother's counter coffee, who was the only, in my opinion, important person to attend her memorial service, she's there, too. She helped my mother stay awake those many nights when Mom knew she had nothing left, but still had the strength to live with that fact, and this woman poured Mom coffee when she sat at the diner counter learning, studying for a test that would never be given, writing a paper that would never be due.

"I have to keep learning," Mom says.

"Come on, get up, get back into bed," I say, but she can't hear me. She stretches her arms out alongside the total history of art. "Did you know all of this existed, Tyrone?"

"Don't call me Tyrone."

"All these books, honey? Look at all of this! I had no idea until today."

"Well, now you know."

"Why am I covered in poo?"

"I don't know. It's a dream. We have to deal with it. Dreams are choosey. Dreams choose you."

"Promise me you won't spend your life trying to get back at your dreams."

I can't hear my response, or even know if I do respond.

The dreamscape changes abruptly.

Now I am banging on a floor, trying to get my downstairs neighbor to shut up. Then there's no banging, no floor, no neighbor, no art, no mom, picture or sound, only an anechoic chamber.

A mahogany mouse, bunnyrabbithopping off a kitchen counter.

I'm startled awake.

Please no mouse.

I'm up for a long time, back to sleep for what feels like a second, and up in time for the early morning darkness.

O

Down on Wall Street, sitting at my desk, I dial our Human Resources Shared Services 24-hour hotline in Bangalore, India to increase my 401K contribution one percentage point. After making my initial request the likely female Bangalorean (voice-altering software makes it difficult to tell; for Bangaloreans, gender is a frequency) asks if I wish to automatically increase my 401K contribution every quarter. Tempted to ask her when she believes quarters occur, I instead respond that that's not necessary at this time.

"Is there anything else I can help you with, sir, help you with, sir, today?"

"Actually, yes. If you have the actuarial tables there, and if you have a second to chat, can you tell me the exact date my father is going to die."

"I am terribly sorry, sir."

"Thanks for that. Do you think you can tell me the exact date my father is going to die. The day, the hour, the time."

Silence.

"Do you have silence in your script?"

"Very much one moment sir of course I can look into that for you."

I feel like I'm practicing robot abuse, the great tacked-on civil rights question of the future, but it makes me feel good to hurt this Bangalorean alien, and I go on.

"Really? I don't know if you can look into it for me. If that question doesn't work for you, can you explain to me when the future April will come? Does it say anything about that in your actuarial tables? This would be the date I would be with my mother again."

Silence.

"Maybe you should look under its Italian name, *in un futuro april.*"

"Let me help you with each request one at a time."

"Certainly I'd be happy to. Do you know the exact date my father is going to die? The day, the hour, the time, the location, how sudden will it be, the cause. Actually I don't need the cause. There's only one cause of death."

Silence.

"Is this something you can help me with?"

"Very much of course one moment sir, please."

"I'll hold," I say.

I hang up.

Midnight Girls, Afternoon Women

Sell when you can—you are not for all markets.
— Shakespeare, As You Like It

Tweed Spreckman helps me develop. He gives me constructive feedback. After meetings, we catch up in the corridors and follow up on immediate next steps. We mute our speakerphones and gossip about the people on the line.

He reminds me I forgot to shave.

As a Navy man, Tweed never forgets to shave.

Every month he treats our strategy team to lunch at Chez Szechuan Phase II, an upscale bistro built over a slave graveyard, they say, just off Cherry Street.

We are a team of sixteen workers who aren't hungry. We send text messages to each other in order to have the conversations we really want, instead of talking to the people sitting right next to us.

We keep our phones in our laps.

There was a time when people kept their phones under the table.

That time is around this time.

I place a napkin on the seat next to mine to save it for Krista Kaplan. When she walks in she brings the confused bistro a Michelin star. Krista is a big girl, the sexiest on our office floor. She wears heels, even on Fridays, and stockings, like in old pictures. In high school I'd have picked her up, on college nights kept her in waters. She isn't frail but her build encourages protection. She has shoulder-length dark hair and polka-dot brown eyes, a large forehead of stillborn pimples. I long to spread my fingers across Krista's temple, douse her pimples with anti-toner, keep her markings as far away as possible from the proven medical ingredients which will shorten their lifespan as blemishes. When I see Krista's pimples I think they're a part of me. When she touches me I not only feel it on my own body, I wonder what it feels like to be her body.

"Sorry, sorry," she says, for being a few minutes late. I remove my napkin from the seat. She sits down, handbag in her lap. Who knows what she might suddenly need?

"It's cool. What were you working on?"

"Let's talk about something else. Anything else. This week sucks."

"Does that stand for Deutsche Bank?" I ask, touching her bag.

"No, Dooney & Bourke," she says, her voice team-oriented, like she just ran off the soccer field.

"I know," I say.

"I know you know."

It's an older woman's bag. Krista carries the handbag for the job she wants, not the job she has.

"I ordered for you, per our discussion."

"Thank you, thank you. I'm starving. Starved."

She hangs her chopsticks over her brown rice. She scoops up seven-and-a-half kernels, samples four of them. She puts her chopsticks down. A few seconds later she picks them up, presses down on a piece of steamed chicken to nudge it in half, chews, swallows. Satiated, she pushes the plate away and sips her ice water.

She uses words like *auspicious, blanched, calendared.* She thinks from different perspectives on items around segmented themes. Her professional self: dry humor, sincere—never sarcastic. Top performers know sarcasm has no value in business.

"You're funny, Ty. But you don't know when to stop being funny."

"At least I'm not as bad as the new guy. Have you met him? He never stops talking about sports."

Michael Mann, our newest associate, and the only black man on our team (there are two black women, and there are the brown stock human figures on our PowerPoint cover sheets) sits at the far end of the table. His head is down in his lap, but I can't tell if he's got a phone in it.

I stare at him until he looks up and meets my eyes.

We share a head nod.

I feel good about myself.

"Yeah I don't want to have anything to do with that," Krista says, interrupting my feelings of peace. "He looks like someone who's going to make your life difficult."

"But not your life," I say, still looking at Michael, whose head is now back down in his lap.

"No. Not my life."

Krista and I share secrets. Off-script winks. Improper conversation during happy hours, whiskey-wet and trading one cigarette between us—*give it to me, give it to me*! And we have our dedicated texting relationship. Even though she claims to hate texting. In private she claims to hate whatever is unstoppable. I like texting, at least with Krista, because with her I feel the pulse of her skin along with her thoughts, and how they sync up to my thoughts. Looking at her makes me a little nervous, but in texting I can be my smartest self, commenting on stuff happening at stoplights, snatches of dialogue I overhear on the street or in the endless drugstore. She writes back, immediately, and I start counting on her quick responses—short, caustic, deep, mean, true. If Krista wants to get it going, she calls it off. If you don't know what it looks like, she doesn't either. If she winks at you during the plenary, she's blowing you during the breakouts.

She moved to New York from the suburbs outside of Detroit. I fictionalize her upbringing in the American interior. She is third-generation American, pure Michigan Jew, first-tier, affluent, admitted early. She studies, learns, has prepped properly from her first spelling test with a three-syllable word. Her high school—land, goalposts, bleachers, track and field, congratulations seniors, father & daughter dance next Tuesday. Her town has a flag football team, sister city not Tokyo like New York but a city to the north, Sapporo maybe, the frosty side of Japan with Russia a refreshing suicide swim away. Cheerleaders and 99.9% acceptance rates. Squads. She bought her yearbook every year and she didn't miss her senior photos because she was stoned, like I did. She never got very stoned, especially when she smoked pot.

But this is true: her mom traveled to Manhattan in the 80s just to see the Met filled with Picassos. She spoke of the old Madison Avenue, the new SoHo; mom had a romantic encounter with Jean-Michel, as she called Basquiat, in the grimy stalls of Danceteria.

Next happy hour it's one cigarette between us and art survey trivia.

"You put on all that cologne and then ruin it with smoking," Krista says.

"I still smell your perfume. I mean, from all the way over here."

Krista doesn't like Renoir. The problem with Renoir is that he never gives you a pussy. She likes Courbet, especially his pussies. "The Origin of the World" is the first thing she views the first time she goes to the Musée d'Orsay when she's 14 years old.

"I have a Courbet," she says.

And she'd love to model for John Currin, in college she sent him nude photos. She doesn't like Schiele. She likes Kokoschka. Schiele is played. Kokoschka isn't.

I search my brain for exhibits around town we could go to. All I can remember is the first retrospective to ever come to America about the way Vikings probably lived.

○

"One of my co-workers is a big art fan," I say to Jenny one night. "You would love this girl."

"The one with the indescribable rack," Jenny says.

"Stop it."

"She's just pretending to like art to sleep with you. She doesn't like art, she likes business."

"She sent nude pictures to Currin. Can you believe that?"

"I can't believe you believed it."

"You said it turns you on when I talk about other girls."

"It does," Jenny says. "So stop doing it."

"What reason would she have to lie about Currin? Who would lie about such a thing?"

"That's what office sluts do, they lie. You lie all the time."

"So do you."

"Fine," Jenny says. "But at least I don't sit in an office all day making you horny."

O

A Philip Guston retrospective comes to the Modern. I go to view Guston's picture of the composer Morton Feldman, and then Jenny and I go, and then I go again, alone, twice. One day I stand in front of it listening to Part 4 of Feldman's composition *For Philip Guston*. The piece goes on for an hour before that, it goes on for hours after it, but it begins and ends with Part 4.

That picture. Guston's portrait of Feldman with the pipe in his mouth. It's the cover photo of Feldman's collected writings, *Give My Regards to Eighth Street*. I go back to the Modern again with Feldman's book, free admission for me and a guest with my corporate perks.

I look at the picture.

I look at the book.

Guston painted the portrait when the two friends didn't like each other. They had an argument over late style. It's like Guston, revenge by way of style, decapitated Feldman using Feldman's head. Everything is red. The picture says red, not green, is the color of jealousy. Feldman's eyes are bloodshot, but also his eyebrows, his plume of cigarette smoke, his Bubblicious forehead and his hair it's all red, with some kind of triangle off to the side of his sideburn that looks menacingly extraterrestrial, like a communication device found on a distant planet that no one can get working again.

This is the problem. There is no longer two-way communication between painter and sitter. That's the most important conclusion I come to while staring at the portrait.

Feldman could be only one man, painted by another man. I want to be one man only, and I want to be alone for just one more hour. But when I'm with a woman—I meet another during one of my solo Guston visits, a petite French tourist with a vintage camera and hip bones like weapons—I think about, during sex, standing not by myself in front of Feldman, but standing with Krista Kaplan in front of Feldman, and I text that to Krista the next time I'm at the exhibit with Jenny.

"Does it have audio guides? I need audio guides, Ty. I can't talk to other people in museums."

Audio guides. Of course. Krista is just the type of person to want an audio guide. To get the ten key bullets in time for the massacre. Audio Guides. Sponsored by Audi. A way to drive yourself around a gallery under luxurious protection. An aid to blocking your eardrums, which is an important sense for seeing a picture. A guide to altering your first impression before heading to the gift shop for an even more distorted second impression.

I wonder what Feldman would've thought of audio guides. As long as it was his music, he probably wouldn't have cared. One of Feldman's central quests was to have no quest, to expel forward motion, ruin associations, ruin the build-up, ruin the character arc, the cross-cross-reference and most of all, to ruin motivation. Motivation is square, one of the devil's tools. The devil is alive in Beethoven. In the Ninth Symphony there is nothing but motivation, nothing but arc: listen to the horse whipping coursing through the *Molto Vivace*. Forward motion is violent motion. Motivation is the heroic brace of war. Feldman's quest was to bury the whip, end the war, spare the horse. And he wrote all of this motivation-free music after the good fight, the good war.

But he failed.

Audio guides won.

Krista Kaplan won.

So did war.

And even before Krista and I have sex she becomes the first woman I think about while having sex with other women—a hood rat, Jenny—even if it's the first time I'm having sex with that woman. This isn't supposed to happen. The whole point of having serial sex partners is to think of nothing but the person in front of me. Now I am thinking about Krista Kaplan. And my thoughts are erotic but also lofty, what we'd be like *after* sex sitting on opposite sides of a dark room, listening to Richard Hawley. All the stuff Jenny and I do together effortlessly and lovingly and, more and more recently, continually.

"Where are you from?" Krista asks.

"Corona."

"Where is that?"

"Queens."

"That sounds really far."

"Where do you live?"

"Fifty-second and Second. I just moved from Fifty-fourth and First."

We're waiting on a short line at the pizza counter. Tweed Spreckman wants us to collaborate on a new project, so we're getting to know each other.

"I want to bring Michael Mann into this project," I say.

"Who?"

"The other new guy. The African-American."

"No, don't," she says.

"It's multi-layered, and he needs to work on something with several dimensions. He needs to learn some new skills so he can finally be self-sufficient."

"You mean you want to bring him in," Krista responds, "so you can have less work."

"Partially. You've got it. Grandma slice, warm," I say to the pizza man.

"It's so cute how you say grandma slice," Krista says, and she puts her hand on my shoulder. She keeps her hand there for some time, long enough for me to glance at it and notice a large ring with a radiant stone. I am reminded of the kryptonite necklace that drowns Superman. For the first time in my life, even though it's not the first time, I feel like I'm cheating on Jenny. The feeling is confusing, mental, but something like physical betrayal, too, and desperation. I know I've lost something sacred.

Krista's hand is still on my shoulder. It's just a slice of pizza. A Grandma slice. A little chopped garlic, olive oil, fresh tomatoes, a sprinkle of basil—a Sicilian slice with Sephardic trimmings.

○

Back in Corona I take Jenny out for pizza and pay with a fifty. I'm using a fifty to impress her.

"Wow," she says. "I should get a topping."

"Get a topping. Get anything you want. Go half-sausage, half-anchovy if your heart so desires. I'm buying. You want a natural soda, too? Garlic knots? Things are going well for me downtown."

"My big strong Wall Street meathead."

"You know it, babe."

Jenny has started showing more and more interest in me, either because she realizes I'm making good money or because she hears me talking so much about Krista, who, even though I helped hire her, is making even more money than me, because she went to a better college and took the salary negotiating class.

Things are going well for Jenny, too. People are starting to notice her work. She publishes a short essay about a father's demise. Dad's death comes as a relief to the female, at least in print. The title "All My Father Gave Me Was Beatings" is a line from *La Dolce Vita* spoken from the backseat of an automobile. She made all this shit up: Jenny's father is healthy and she loves him like crazy. The essayist Jenny Marks is not the dour urban citizen she scapegoats in her writing. Her idea of a cosmopolitan afternoon is watching prosecutorial Italians lob bocce balls in the sand lot behind The Lemon Ice King of Corona. But her essay is true, deeply felt and fully observed, and her editor is amazed, thinks the piece so honest, very brave, tells her to send him anything.

"Go deeper into your voice," he tells her.

Her next essay, titled "His Ideas," introduces photographs. A man (me) takes a weekend sex romp a step too far and forces a woman to eat an entire boiled chicken. The story runs alongside time-stamped photos of Jenny's face covered in (my) semen. The editor is even more amazed. Jenny took his suggestion to go deeper into her voice. He blasts the link to everyone he knows and doesn't know. Jenny earns mentions, a devoted editor—the only person more important to a writer than the parents from the unhappy childhood—and she earns a following among people who all know each other and have the same devoted editor.

"The thing is, I don't know any of them," she says. "But I'm also not totally convinced they know each other."

"I mean it must be legit, right? They all have email addresses."

"Oh yeah."

"You need a manager."

"An agent, you mean."

"Yeah. Someone with access who gets a cut."

○

Down on Wall Street I spend long hours at the office, getting ahead. Jenny picks me up late one Friday night and we drive to Brooklyn for one of her famous book parties.

After I get in the car I ask, "How many of the guys at this party will you have slept with? How many of these guys gave you all of the blistering content for your brave essay?"

"Too high to count."

"These guys, my spunk."

"Where's your office slut? With the indescribable rack."

Krista Kaplan is still at her desk, working, getting even further ahead than me. "Stop it," I say. "Why do you suddenly care who I sleep with?"

"That's what you called them."

"What?"

"Her breasts. The other night. You used the word *indescribable*. I associate that word with famine, not body parts. I associate that word with a hospice nurse, not an office slut's body work. You were drunk."

"So were you."

"I knew this was going to happen. I knew you were going to meet some fake Ohio slut when you started working down here."

"She's from Michigan, actually."

I have a present for Jenny, the drawings of Lee Lozano, her favorite artist. The book cost a fortune at Borders and if I didn't start working downtown, I think to myself, I never could have gotten it for her. She thanks me but she doesn't seem to care. We kiss again, her tongue is hot, she places the book in the backseat and floors the gas. I also bought myself a present, a Brahms CD. It's the Rubinstein recording of the C-Minor Piano Quartet. The first notes are just a C octave. It could very well be a C-Major Piano Quartet. In fact, it's been suggested that only Rubinstein can touch this octave and signal to the listener that the pending chord will indeed be in the minor. That suggestion is a bit dramatic.

"What do you think?" I ask. "Decadent. Sinful. Do you like it?"

"Sounds like a chocolate commercial."

We make it to Brooklyn and park Big Red on Bedford Avenue. Jenny affixes the Club to the steering wheel as if it can actually stop theft. She is in her usual mood, nervous and also pissed-off. She wears paint-stained jeans, white sneakers, a heather-gray sweatshirt with a mustard stain. I remember the hot dog it came from. There's a wine stain above her heart. I remember uncorking the bottle.

"If we could take two feet of this shit back to Queens," she says, looking up and down Bedford Avenue, "we'd never have to leave Queens. Or excuse me, I'd never have to."

"It doesn't matter," I say. "We own everything."

Middle-aged artists, poor, bodega credit, dimensional community. Younger artists, cinched outfits, big belts, black cars to Delancey Street.

Jenny takes little steps up and down the street to sniff out No Parking restrictions. We walk toward the party building on the East River, which isn't even a real river but rather a saltwater tidal strait.

The main door of the building, jimmied open with wads of aluminum foil, has a note that says UP, UP, UP! The stairwell is hot with sudden bursts of coldness that don't blow out of vents. We climb flight after flight of creaking stairs, passing illegal dwellings undergoing domestication.

The crowd is smart and thick. I offer my name without being asked. I pour bourbon in a plastic cup. I look for the guy Jenny was falling in love with, the guy who roughed her up, the guy who believes the American family is a state of mind, the guy whose trench coat she was wearing the night we drove to the airport. I don't think that piece of shit is at the party. He's not really the party kind of guy, he's the stay-in-his-room kind of guy, work-on-his-poetry kind of guy.

"You need a day job right now," another guy says. I remember him from college, a Classics survey. He asked the professor if vegetables were grown in Homer's time.

"Maybe," I respond. "But the day job is just my job, you know? It's what I do all day and what I think about all night."

Every twenty minutes the party gets louder than it was twenty minutes before. A different guy Jenny slept with, beanie nudged up on his balding skull, says he recognized my ejaculate on her essay. "Congratulations," he says. "Your semen is a part of history."

I escape to the big window and light a cigarette. Icons of Buddha, Shiva and Mary rest on a triangular wooden table. Two women find my window to smoke their own cigarettes. I don't recognize them, but sense that Jenny would. They fit on the ledge knee-to-knee, smoke and discuss the gods on the table. Their excitable talk suggests they too are writers like Jenny, and they have millions of ideas, but not "His Ideas".

"What's uglier," one says, gesturing out the window, "Jesus or that building?"

I ask, "Do you think I look conventional?"

"Usually people who are conventional don't think they are."

"I mean, I came from Wall Street. I'm wearing a suit."

"I've never been at a party where more straight dudes cared what they look like."

"I'm overdressed, right? Do you think I look like Luigi the plumber, but dressed up? Like for Mario's funeral."

"Totally," one of them says.

"You look really Catholic," the other adds. "Like the dude in *My Night at Maud's.*"

"How do you know I'm not gay? You don't even know me."

"Because," she says, sniffing coke from her key, "sometimes straight white dudes think they're gay because it's the only way they have left to be different."

"I'm not exactly a white dude, I'm an Ashkenphardic-Sicilian."

"Whatever, nigga."

Maybe she's right, I think to myself, sniffing the last of the blow off her key. Because what's Ashkenphardic-Sicilian? What's Italian? A Torani squirt? A coffee roast darker than French? What's Italian? If Giuliani's Italian, I don't want to be. Fascists? Peasants? People who can recite *Goodfellas*? Using a spoon to eat pasta and asking for a fork at a sushi place? Mario's mustache? That's not Italian, it's the Japanese coding oliveface. And what's a Jew, anyway? What's Jewish? Choosing yoga over wine? I wanna go to Florida? Asking a lot of questions? If you're not wailing at the wall or beating your breast in the temple, what are you Jewish for? Scots-Irish lox on your bagel? If Mike Bloomberg is Jewish, I don't want to be. Naming your daughter Krista instead of Leah? What's

Jewish? Hating on Hezbollah to the North and Hamas to the South? Siding with Woody Allen, sidestepping the troubling stuff in Dostoyevsky, spending your whole life trying to figure out why Shylock's daughter is such a coward? Is it more difficult to choose a God or choose a cuisine? Well, what am I in the mood for? I've got the money to buy Jenny large pizzas for the rest of our earthly lives. I think I'll start with ten pretzels, ten hot dogs, ten hot sausages drowned in soupy onions, strawberry-lime fruit bars, and two orders of anything filled with cheddar cheese. I want basmati rice, tandoori lamb, lot of white sauce, lot of red. I want seven lightly toasted salt bagels with vegetable, chive n' onion and lox cream cheese, each with two tomato slices, a large jar of half-sour pickles, quarter-pound whitefish salad, half-a-pound of Muenster, and I want garlic knots, a large grape soda from an Enjoy Coke fountain, a Grandma slice, from the corner, give me the one on the corner.

Jenny walks toward the big window. She has a real rocks glass instead of a plastic cup. She always finds the real glasses at parties. She sucks the last of bourbon off her ice. The two girls stand from the window ledge, congratulate Jenny on the bravery of her essays and walk back to the party. Jenny tells them she loves their essays, too.

"You know what I think is indescribable? The bravery of your essays."

"Say it like in Salinger."

"God dammit. You know what *I* think is inde*scrib*able? The bravery of your *essays*, for Christ's sake."

"I'd kill for some boiled chicken right about now."

"Well, let's get out of here."

Our goodbyes make me burn with love and wonder for what I didn't say, any conversation I missed, everything I didn't open myself up to, whatever it is I didn't learn.

On the walk back to the car, my mind reinterprets the cocaine I snorted off the girl's key. Bubbled-up, autumnal drip, sticky buds on the bare rod of my throat. I play air-double-bass when I hear "Don't Sweat the Technique" from a second-story window.

"Don't collaborate with that girl in your office anymore," Jenny says.

"Stop it. It's not even like that. And you have no right to say that to me. You turned out every Ohio dude at that party and you chose *my* semen for the permanent record?"

"Eric's from Iowa, actually. Your meathead semen was the most photogenic, Ty."

In the car, we polish off the boiled chicken. Some grease hits the Lee Lozano retrospective. The chicken looks like so much chicken until we get down to the final pieces of meat and have to portion it out POW-style. I find a bag of unsalted bodega almonds in the glove compartment.

"Why would you ever buy unsalted almonds?"

Jenny scrounges up a few McDonald's salt packets from the cup holder and we try, unsuccessfully, to salt the almonds. I give up and hand her the bag. She asks me to hold it and feed her almonds as she drives drunk over the bridge.

"I knew you were going to meet a corporate slut from Ohio once you started being fake."

"Fully chew your almond. Again, she's from Michigan. And she has a Courbet."

"Don't move to the city."

"I'll never leave Queens, babe, not really. I'm having déjà vu right now. Wait, it's gone."

"I'm never leaving my parents," Jenny says. "I can think of nothing cornier than leaving your parents."

"Because you live for free and don't have to work."

"That's not the only reason."

"Maybe there's something to be said for that."

"What does that mean?"

"That's what folks always say when they talk about living close, right, how we all live so far apart for the first time in 500,000 years. They say, maybe there's something to be said for that. But what is it? What is it that's being said?"

"There is something to be said."

"It's the only thing about you I don't understand."

"It's not."

"It's easy to lay around at home under the blankets and watch the same old shows. You never need to actually say anything, or feel vulnerable and learn something new. You never need to talk."

"That's why I love it."

"You know what your favorite artist Lee Lozano said? Why do you need roots when you have gravity? Tell me, why do we need roots when we have gravity!"

I make a move toward the book in the backseat.

"Just leave it. Why are you trying to hurt me? Why are you always yelling at me?"

"I'm not. You're the most radical person in every other way. You tricked those Brooklyn kids into thinking you're brave. You have a responsibility to charge ahead and stab them with a spear straight through the heart."

I reach for her hand, she grabs mine until I realize she needs both for her driving. "Why are we driving right now?"

"I'm driving."

"Why are you driving right now? You're drunk."

I think to myself, *this is a bad idea, this is a bad idea, this is a bad idea*, but we make it back to Corona, park and smoke two more cigarettes.

"Come up," I say.

"You're sure? Because I'm not, Ty, I'm not sure. I might leave after."

"That's fine. But first you have to come up. If you want to."

"Midnight girls, afternoon women," Jenny says. "That's what my aunt always called it."

"Which one are you?"

"Both."

We go to my bedroom and have sex on the floor so that the headboard doesn't disturb my father.

"What's that noise?" Jenny asks. "That's insane."

"It's this guy Juan, the new boarder. He's very passionate."

"Your Dad sleeps through that?"

"He's very passionate."

After sex, we go back to the bed. Jenny says she's going to stay for just a few minutes. Then she says, "You didn't know my block."

"I'm sure it was a lot like my block. It's all the same block. We all grew up on the same block."

"Hardly. You didn't know my block."

"Who says *hardly*?"

"I do. After midnight, before dawn, when I'm in bed with you."

Jenny tells me about baseball games on her block. The pitcher stood in the middle of the street, the batter on the sidewalk, and behind the pitcher, on the opposite sidewalk, defenders. Two houses were in fair territory, including Jenny's house, and whenever she hit a home run off her own house she felt a mix of pride for her batting power and relief for not breaking her father's windows.

She liked pitching more. The pitcher had a particular advantage on her block. The batter stood against a fence, and the pitcher could use the No Parking sign on that fence as her automatic strike. Aiming for that high and inside No Parking sign encouraged dangerous pitching, and whenever balls sailed over the fence the old man who owned the house refused to throw them back. He never mellowed. He kept his bushes pruned, the grass trimmed no-nonsense like his crew cut. Even Jenny's father tried to reason with him because he got tired of buying the block new balls.

One summer, right after July 4th, Jenny broke her foot. Feet, they never heal. They're notorious for that. Jenny couldn't walk at first. She could only paint five of her toenails. She had to watch games from her stoop, acting as a kind of designated and stationary centerfielder in case a homerun happened to fall right in her lap. She learned too much from that stoop, repetitions from those days, hair braiding from her friend Unique, one day blending into the next. She read books all afternoon and all through the night. She learned to wait, that's what she learned, when she broke her foot. The next summer she didn't pitch at all.

"Injury is another routine, like health is another routine. You know that quote? Two sides of the same river."

"Wellness is Queens, Sickness is Manhattan."

"Correcto. And that's when my impingement first started acting up."

"What's that? What's an impingement?"

"It's a shoulder problem. It's painful."

"I'll help you stay pinged," I say, and at that moment I really believe it. We fall asleep. It's a romantic leap in our relationship that we only had sex once and didn't feel the need to order a pizza.

In the morning, I wake up to the sight of Jenny staring out my window.

"Look! A golden-winged ship is passing my way. I love how straight they are," she says, commenting on my baseball caps. Hung on nails, they line up below the window. My girl tries my Mets cap on, she tries my SF Giants cap on. "My meathead. Why Giants? Because the Cali teams were made by the breakup of the old New York teams?"

"Yes, scholar."

"I could strike you out," Jenny says. "You didn't see me pitch on my block, Ty, I was simply the best. Dwight Gooden would call me for tips."

"You mentioned last night," I say, leaving the room to piss. When I return I see Jenny sniffing the brim of my Dodger's cap.

"What are you doing?"

"Smelling you."

"I never wear that one. You're smelling Foot Locker."

○

For the next few days I'm really sick. Ear, nose and throat, a severe case of the relationships.

"What year is it?" I ask Jenny.

"2003.144444444444444…."

She goes to the drugstore for me, buys me the name-brand cold and flu medicine. I climb back into bed, hide under my redeeming comforter, sleep for twelve hours, and when I wake up the waves of sickness still crash inside me. I send Dad away. I tell Jenny to stay away, but it seems like she's moved in. I need drugs every four hours, bowls of steaming soup. Jenny brings me the *Post* and magazines. She calmly predicts my return to full strength. She reads me to me from *Illness as Metaphor*, in a New York Intellectual accent: *Illness is the night-side of life, a more onerous citizenship. Everyone who is born holds dual citizenship, in the kingdom of the well and in the kingdom of the sick. Although we all prefer to use only the good passport, sooner or later each of us is obliged, at least for a spell, to identify ourselves as citizens of that other place.*

"I feel so sick. I think my body lives in Brooklyn."

"A more onerous citizenship."

"That's it," I say. "I am in the kingdom of the sick right now. My good body moved to Brooklyn for a few days. Soon, it will show its healthy passport and return to Queens."

Jenny edges closer, consumes my excess heat.

"I'll need to go home and make some more chicken."

"Make it here," Dad tells her.

With a new chicken in the pot, and me using the steam of the shower to clear up my breathing, Dad and Jenny become friends. He lets her put on a Hitchcock movie.

"Wow, what happened to *Superman*?" I ask.

"Jennifer brought this over," Dad says. "He's the godfather of suspense."

"When you get better Ty, we'll have a picnic lunch. Yes that's right, a picnic lunch. I'll pack a picnic lunch of some cold chicken and beer. And I'll bring a salt shaker so we can salt the chicken."

She comes into my bedroom, crawls into bed with me. "Stay away!" I tell her. "You're going to get what I've got!"

"Too late," she says into my fever-warm shoulder. "Sometimes when we're together I feel like it's a roller coaster, and I'm all strapped in, I know I'm going be safe, but then you come over, you're that creep from Ireland working for the summer at Morey's Pier, you push the bar down and it hurts my legs. It really hurts, Ty."

"Stop it," I say. "I'm sick."

"You didn't know my block," Jenny answers.

"It was all the same block."

"One day you'll meet another me and the new me won't be me and that's going to suck for me until one day it's going to suck for you because you'll realize your new wife is just me and you'll howl for how you hurt me."

"Come on."

"You were meant to be with a me. I just hope it's me."

○

I'm all better, and we leave the house and ride the R train into the city. We start walking toward Central Park.

"This neighborhood is making me queasy," Jenny says. "Bragosaurus after bragosaurus."

"I don't know if I'll be allowed inside the park," I say.

"What do you mean?"

"Well of course I'm allowed but I mean, I don't think I have the key."

"We'll find a twig and put it in the lock."

"Okay. That's what I need. Let's look for the twig. I just don't want there to be a force field, you know. Sometimes I think they'll be a force field keeping me out of the park. I need a level-seven whistle or something."

We walk freely through the open gates of the park. On the paths and benches we see musicians, shrewd portrait painters, undercover cops, Lycee students hogging love. A father replies, to the girl up on his shoulders, *well we don't have these types of clouds in California, sweetie.*

Jenny stops walking at the North Fields. We leave the path and head to the baseball diamond. Two tall men are moving slowly and practicing bunting.

"These guys must be serious. Who bunts anymore?"

"I can strike you out here," Jenny says.

Jenny explains our needs to the men. They laugh, offer us their equipment. They walk over to the dugout and sit down on the bench to watch us. Jenny trots over to me and hands me a bat, keeps a scuffed ball and mitt for herself.

"This is like Eckersley's glove in '85 Topps," she says, obviously impressed with herself. She pounds the glove with the ball and walks out to the mound.

I walk to home plate. I look out and study my Corona girl on the mound. Ponytail through her cap, my girl comes out of the stretch overhand, nasty, upfront. On her glove hand an exposed middle finger, flipping off an unseen runner at third. Around her, Manhattan emptiness. She has no opposition below the power lines.

As for me, I feel past my prime. I check the make of the bat, Louisville Slugger, and let it rest on my left shoulder. From the batter's box I realize how large a baseball field is, how far away I stand from the imaginary fences. This is the one setting from childhood that never gets smaller. I crouch, cock, pretend to have a stance, it is my lump of information, the ways I've watched dozens of hitters stand before. I have no style of my own.

Jenny stomps the dirt. Her clothes suit the dirt.

"I always forget we're both lefties," I yell to her. "Except with scissors, right?"

"And I iron right," she says. She turns around to her imaginary fielders. I watch her big boxy ass. How animal her back is, how unprotected. She pounds her mitt and circles the mound. I never want to let her win. I want to hit a home run. We have no defense. That means a home run will be anything over Jenny's head. All I have to do is make contact.

"I hope this doesn't make my impingement act up," she says.

"What about your foot?"

"Feet, they never heal."

"Yeah, they're notorious for that."

"What doesn't heal stops bothering you, eventually."

Jenny delivers her first pitch, overhand, fast, straight until it curls inside. I swing and miss, feel a pull in my lower back.

"Strike one," I say, but Jenny plays it off like it's not a thing. She reaches behind her for an imaginary bag of chalk. I go to the backstop and throw the ball back. She looks at it, making sure she doesn't have to request a new ball from an unknown ump. She walks back to the mound and falls into her set position, checking runners on the deserted bases before coming into her wind-up and delivering another fast pitch.

This one doesn't curve, it rises, and my bat rises with it, but not enough.

"Strike two!"

I throw the ball back. Jenny returns to the mound and holds the glove up to her face, covering it, so an imaginary runner at second base won't be able to see where she places her fingers on the seams, then she steps off the mound and walks in a circle.

"In case my impingement acts up I want to give the bullpen time to get loose."

"Your impingement is going to stay pinged."

"You're down 0-2, Tyrone. You've got to protect the plate. Why don't you choke up a little?"

She goes through her motions and delivers the pitch. It starts off in what I think is my sweet spot, I really think I'm going to belt it out, I'm going to win this battle, but the pitch ends up in the dirt and I swing so hard I fall down crying.

Jenny walks slowly toward the plate until she's standing over me. "You're out," she whispers.

I raise my hand up, giving her the opportunity to lend hers.

"I hope that made you feel better," I say, standing up on my own.

Jenny says she didn't feel bad before.

O

Bloomfield Hills. Ann Arbor. Summer in western Europe. Magical, perspective-shifting summer in Israel, an adventurous daytrip to Jordan's beaches. Bloomfield Hills for a few weeks. A family friend's coach house in Port Jefferson, Long Island. Fifty-second and Second. Fifty-fourth and First.

Krista Kaplan celebrates her latest move by throwing what she calls, in her subject line, a Studiowarming.

"I'm really only inviting people from work," she says. "I don't know anyone else in the city."

"Did you send the invite to Michael?" I ask. "He told me he's been feeling left out of social stuff."

"It's not a big thing, just a few people."

"I'm not in the mood for a get-together."

"Whatever, puppy, I'll text you after."

I sit at home that night, watching the game with Dad. I delay responding to Krista's text pulse. I must when she writes, *this isn't like you.* In the game, the camera settles on a girl in the stadium seats. There's no reason for the camera to be on her for that long. She's unaware she's being filmed, until her friend nudges her, and then she waves at her own face on the Jumbotron like the ship is leaving port.

"She's good looking," Dad says.

"That's the only reason they put her on screen," I say.

"Every man's dream."

I clear his plates and wash his dishes, setting them in the slats of the drying rack. I heat up my own dinner of fully-cooked extra-lean chicken strips. When I hear the strips crackling I toss in red pepper parts and broccoli florets. By the time everything is ready nothing is hot. I eat the lukewarm dish standing against the sink. After wiping my plate clean, a fork stumbles into the garbage disposal, tines up. I position my neck over the drain, zero in on the tines, my finger hovering over the disposal switch. If I switch up, will the fork fly in my face? What speed is disposal-miles-per-hour?

Jenny sends me a message, asking if I want to hang out.

I don't message her back.

"I have to go to a party in Midtown," I tell my father.

"You *have* to go to a party in Midtown?"

"It's a work thing, I've got to go."

○

Krista's new place on Fifty-fourth and First is an old walk-up with rehab hopes. In the lobby there's a shuttered antique shop. To tease tenants about improvements, a dying plant is added to the dark hallway. Above that plant, a framed Mark Rothko print. It's hung crooked, the picture hanger just gave up, like the Stieglitz prints in our office conference rooms. There are new apartment buzzers, too. One has a note: ALREADY DOESN'T WORK.

The party is over. Krista's apartment is near-dark but the alcohol shines. There's no real closet and below the windows I notice a hand-painted chest where she must keep her hot-girl clothes. There's clutter, glasses and cups left over from the Studiowarming.

"If you would've come," she says, "the party would've worked."

"It's not your fault. House parties are hard in Manhattan."

"It works in *Breakfast at Tiffany's*."

"Yeah but that's a movie. In real life you need huge tracts of land to throw even the simplest party. You need causes and donors for intimate get-togethers. You spearhead a foundation, basically, just to play poker."

On a small table I notice a laminated placemat of the U.S. capitals, the state flowers and other key facts. Cheese is from Wisconsin, money from Nevada, syrup from Vermont.

"I'm bad with the capitals. I'm trying to learn."

"Good for you," I say, thrilled there's something Krista Kaplan doesn't know how to do. "I don't think I know the capitals from school, you know. My Dad taught me them."

"My Dad didn't," she says.

"What's New Jersey?"

"Trenton?"

I say nothing.

"Come on. Is it Trenton?"

"We've reached that moment when talking doesn't make much sense."

"Let's stop talking then."

"No I mean I must text someone."

"I love a man with his own hobbies," Krista says.

Jenny had sent me a message with two question marks. I respond that I've got to wake up early, work is killing me and I'm going to bed.

Krista and I walk up to her roof to have a glass of wine. The sign on the door says EMERGENCY ALARM WILL SOUND. It doesn't. We stand on the roof, looking out on real estate I will never own.

"Communication is the hobby of the future," I say.

"Let me hold your phone. I want to see the model."

She compares my phone to her phone. We have a long discussion on the pros and cons of keeping work and personal data in different phones. She touches my chest, circles an area with one finger. We share the same taxpayer I.D. We share a Dun & Bradstreet number. We kiss. I don't know. It's not what I thought. I don't feel the warmth I do with Jenny, but sometimes, I reason, it's hot to be cold. A part of me believes that Jenny can see us kissing through my phone. We kiss deeper, and I start thinking about how fingerprint technology lags behind, like electric car technology. Passwords are weak, fingerprints are strong. Capital craves security breaches, to create murmurs and fluctuations in stock prices and scare users into believing the world is a dangerous place. I'm there, I've got it, and now I see business news figureheads but instead of economic trends coming out of their mouths they are fire-breathing dragons.

"Maybe we shouldn't do this," I say, moving away.

"Okay," Krista says. "It makes no difference to me."

"It makes no difference to you?"

"You're the one who made the move."

"You started touching my chest. I think that's a move."

"You still made the first move."

"I'm not sure that's true. I think I'm going to go home."

"Don't *think* you're going to go home, just go home."

"I'm going home."

"So go home. You don't have to stop being yourself when you're with me. Be yourself, just let me in on it."

"Got it," I answer, like I'm taking orders at work.

○

The Yankees win the Series and the world doesn't care. Halloween decorations are up in the bay windows of brownstones, the commercial windows of drugstores. I run my fingers through the orange and black streamers of a Halloween store. A tarantula made of black pipe cleaners, red stones for eyes, clings to the front gate. A life-sized burn victim, a vintage California Raisin. These temporary businesses make me think of Halloween as a traveling holiday. It happens in New York on October 31st. Then, the store moves to Cincinnati, where Halloween takes place on November 2nd.

We attend a spooky-themed happy hour in Midtown, a few blocks from Krista's apartment. We aren't dressed up. No one else is either.

"Let's go downtown," Krista says.

She hails the taxi and two guys stop for her. She smells both cars and picks the freshest. She tells the driver to go down to West Fourth Street. We kiss, a little skirt, our taxi romance. With my arm around her photogenic shoulder I guide her eyes out the window to take note of the implacable man in the moon.

When we get out of the taxi, someone punches me in the eye with an apple. I am okay, I am okay, for ten minutes. It's a real shock, I have to say.

Every bar overflows with students and revelers. We choose the emptiest. The jukebox becomes our personal stereo. We nudge tables and chairs so we can dance. We trade bumps with an unimpressive stockbroker. He's proof that passing the Series 7 & 63 is only exciting in the movies. For his costume, he holds a Jason mask under his arm.

The bartender is the villain Rooster from *Annie.* At the end of the bar sits an underage Miss Hannigan, nursing a tall glass of clear alcohol.

"What are you guys?" Miss Hannigan sulks.

"We're people from Midtown," Krista says.

"Midtown hood rats," I say. "We rarely leave."

"Why is this place empty?" Krista asks Rooster.

"Because it smells like puke," Miss Hannigan says.

"Where are your orphans?" Krista asks Miss Hannigan.

"They're around here somewhere," Miss Hannigan says.

Krista turns to me. "Why did you use that word, hood rat?"

"Because I'm from Queens."

"Words matter. People aren't vermin."

"Words don't matter," I say. "Money matters."

"Do I look like a rat?" Krista asks.

"I love it when you Americans come to New York and tell us we don't talk good."

Krista asks Rooster the name of the movie on the muted TV.

"*Stranger Than Paradise*," he crows. He unplugs the jukebox and turns up the TV. We watch the heartbreaking final act, which chronicles a simple miscommunication between friends in 20th century Florida.

Rooster restarts the jukebox. Krista and Miss Hannigan dance together. Laughing orphans run out from behind the bar to join them.

"Do you own Apple stock?" the trader asks me.

"No, but I was just punched in the eye with an apple."

"Apple is on fire," he says. "I'll give you $3,000 to make out with your girlfriend."

"She's not my girlfriend."

Krista comes over and says, "Miss Hannigan is such a good dancer."

The trader tries to kiss Krista for free. She has to push him away. I threaten him. He produces a plastic machete that he's been hiding underneath his trench coat. Then he takes a real *West Side Story*-looking knife out of his back pocket. We're all stunned, and then we recover. Rooster pummels him. The trader wobbles up, affixes his Jason mask and storms after all of us. We step aside just as he crashes into the jukebox.

O

Kill em' all. I hope you die. At happy hours, none of us have to watch our mouths anymore. Death to entire families. The hippie aunt in Taos. The Navy man from Ft. Worth now living in San Diego. The day laborer blowing leaves from the lawns of Chicago's North Shore. The industrial worker in southeastern Ohio, prepping for his *New Yorker* expose in their "Voices Of The American Interior" double issue. The wind farm workers of inner Mongolia sliced into tiny pieces. The undecided voter decided by a massive brain hemorrhage. The Recovering Cajun, a Creole alcoholic who flees to Metairie.

"Or is it the Recovering Creole, a Cajun alcoholic who flees to Metairie?"

"I am horrible, right?" Krista says.

"I don't know why it continues to surprise you."

We're at a bar in Midtown that will be better once everyone else leaves. A friend of Krista's shows up and orders a white wine. Luanne is tiny, wears big black-rimmed glasses. She takes layers off down to a V-neck undershirt. She just moved to New York from Hong Kong's Kowloon District, where her father owns a commercial real estate brokerage. We have a long discussion on the tiers of cities. What makes a city truly global? We come to the conclusion that New York City is the Portland, Oregon of Hong Kong and Zingerman's Deli is the Austin, Texas of the state of Michigan. Then we discuss graphic design and documentary filmmaking until a moment of silence confirms we have little in common with Luanne.

Krista and I go to the bar. She orders two shots, herself a vodka tonic. "Do you like Luanne? I really admire how she's following her dreams."

"Yeah, me too. I don't meet a lot of people who follow their dreams."

"We're both each other's first friends in the city, so we'll always have that bond."

"Nice."

"I keep waiting for something amazing to happen to me in New York."

"What about what's happening to you right now? I mean, daily life is the most amazing thing there is."

"The city is empty right now."

"There are probably more people on their overnight lunch hours right now than every worker in the entire state of Ohio."

I read a plaque on the paneling: When ancient man screamed and beat the ground with sticks they called it WITCHCRAFT. When modern man does the same thing, they call it GOLF.

"Maybe you should learn to play golf," I say to Krista.

"I know how. Soda now not tonic," she slurs at the bartender. She holds her drink in one hand and waves her phone in the other. She sniffs a lot, coke, not a cold. When she takes a breath she says, "You're flirting with me, Ty, but you don't make a move."

"Why is it necessary to make a move? When you say that, that's a move. I mean when you say 'Why don't you make a move, Ty,' you're making a move."

"You keep asking leading questions."

"We're making conversation."

"A star knows when she's being interviewed. You care about me."

"Of course I do," I say to the bar. "We're colleagues."

The bartender comes back with our drinks and waters.

"What do we look like?" Krista asks.

The bartender studies me. I hold a false smile. She says to Krista, "Like you've known him for six minutes or six years."

○

The driver starts the meter before we pull away. It doesn't bother me as much as it usually does. Krista puts a big smile on her face, her sharp cheeks stressed, teeth easygoing like old friends, and she quickly turns that big smile into an exaggerated frown. I try to imitate her, fail, and we laugh. She does it again. When her mouth loses all expression I move closer. I place my hand above her knee, on a long stem of her stocking's roses.

I hesitate at her door, acting.

"Stop it," she says. "You know you're coming up. Unless you have to run home again?"

We go up. I sit on the edge of her bed. Krista gets down on her knees and smiles up at me.

"You need to make the first move," she says.

"What are you doing right now?" I ask.

"You're the boy," she says, unzipping my pants.

"Yeah but you've made every single other move, so what number move am I actually making right now?"

"First."

"I don't think you really believe that. I mean, what number move does my first move end up? I'm not like this with anyone else but you. This is not how I am."

"I want you to make the first move," she says.

"See, that's another move."

"Bigger," she says.

"This is pretty big."

"I know you've got more, Ty."

"See, that's a move. We e-file using the same Federal Tax I.D., receive the same W-2s."

"I make more money than you, puppy."

Now that's my baby. She's knocking on my door. She's my baby and my baby will never lose, she'll never lose that knock, she'll never lose those hips, I'm going to make sure she always has her walker. She'll mash my bananas when my teeth turn to gums and place my pills in seven-day containers. She'll extract my saw palmetto and withhold judgment when my chest turns to soy. She'll never stop staring up at me with the eyesight of broken institutions. Oh there's my baby. She's looking right up at me. I don't know what she sees, but it's not me. I don't have a name. I don't have a face. Over my face is a premium bubble. I am protected I am the face value of unlimited semen, my fluids flip abandoned properties. There's my baby and her mitochondrial eve is my Carthaginian peace.

"You like that?"

"I do."

Yeah. I'll come home from a hard day's work right before you come home from an even harder day's work. Things will no longer be in the place we left them—the joy of cohabitation. I'll pour myself one spirit mix it equal parts with another. I'll toss salad in a bamboo bowl and watch balsamic droplets glisten on tri-colored leaves. We will decide to eat on the couch instead of the dining room table. We will press play and wait for the movie to start.

"You want me to keep going?"

"You can."

"You want me to keep going?"

"I do."

Just be careful. Remember that cheerleading is an American invention. Never forget that. Americans invented cheerleading. And philanthropy. Just be careful. Be smart. Don't go doing any adoring right now. Krista is not the kind of girl you want to put in your basket and head to market all adoring. What kind of *Kaplan* names their kid *Krista*, anyway? Is her stepmom's name Amber Greenstein-Kaplan? Be careful. Otherwise, I'll end up apologizing for this blow job. I'm sorry I came. I'm sorry I love you. I'm sorry these aren't in first class. She gets off accepting apologies. All beauties do.

"What's the capital of Maryland?"

"Baltimore?"

"Wrong! Wrong! Wrong!"

Oh there's my baby. And I'm her upmarket man. I miss the holes. The old holes. When holes were holes. Who will pen folk songs for the departed gash? This hole was your hole, this hole was my hole. Now I've got no name. Now I've got no face. My erasure is my glory. No chit-chat, no pardon, no parole. Oh there's my baby. Make a full sky of clouds now. Pour endless rain. Bar-raised pole vaulter concussed, cipher a vandalized zygote. Scope me from your tower, meet me in the mountains, avoid me in the streets. He who has no name is a godless herd.

○

I go over to Krista's every night after work that week. I know I'm coming up whenever I'm coming up. That's what we do—we invite each other up. I also trick myself into believing that because I'm sleeping with a girl in Midtown, I can afford to live in Midtown.

"Quick, what's the capital of Vermont?"

"Burlington."

"Wrong! Montpelier."

"Montpelier," she says, like she's wearing dinner gloves instead of her gym clothes. A natural flush enhances her self-tanner. She wears black leggings and there's a racetrack window of leg between them and her pink socks, which match her cross-trainers and their pink laces which match the pink of her t-shirt, a reddish-pink earth from a day of community service.

"Quiet," she says. "I turned around today at the gym and caught this guy looking at me. He reminded me of you. He looked like he wanted to set me on fire. Do you want to set me on fire, puppy?"

"What's the use. I don't think you'd burn."

She screams, too, but her scream fades, mine intensifies, my scream is better, easier to believe in, my scream wins. What do I have to lose in the moments leading up to this? Soon enough I will be eaten for taste, imprisoned for observation, tested for product, hunted for management, adored for companionship, my sexual organs excised. Only the shrew, the circular breather plugged into a sexual respirator, escapes. She screams, but not like me. Krista rolls over during my scream and in her female fallback tone of temperance says, "Alright, puppy, that's enough. My neighbors are going to think you're strangling me."

"Kaplan," I sigh. "Don't you tell me what's enough. Don't you tell me what's enough."

"See, that's a move."

Bobby D.

Though I speak with the tongues of men and of angels, and have not charity, I am becoming as sounding brass, or a tinkling cymbal.
— 1 Corinthians 13:1 (KJB)

We're going to fire our only African-American male associate, Michael Mann. Tweed Spreckman taps me to run point on the termination. I calendar meetings, leave a paper trail, take notes in a Business Notebook made by Cambridge Stationers. I transcribe my notes into an email and send them to Tweed, who files them in a disciplinary action folder, a duplicate copy of which I also keep in a hanging file with a cc: to Krista Kaplan.

We do this for weeks.

"To fire a black man," Tweed says, "you must overwrite."

It's all my fault. I was the one who hired him. Things have been going badly. Michael is focusing on all the wrong stuff. He tells me that the fruit cups we give out at breakfast meetings make him depressed. I tell him the fruit cups were not the prime focus of his new job. He says, the grapes in these cups are so wilted, coach.

We're standing in the commons area near the ancient microwave.

"This grape makes me feel lazy like Snoopy," Michael says. "This job just gets me down sometimes, coach. I feel like Tweed's slave sometimes."

"Well, you are Tweed's slave. We're all slaves here. Welcome to the world of consulting."

"You feel like a slave, too?"

"Of course. We're all Spreckman's slaves. Or you're Spreckman's caddy. If you screw up, you're misclubbing him. When the partners look at you they don't see a human being, just like they don't see cows in their steaks. They're entitled to you, same as they're entitled to their porterhouse."

"Yeah, but he's never interested in my ideas," Michael says. "And I thought we were supposed to be creative. Today he told me his strategy, and I told him my opinion, and he got pissed off and gave me busy work."

"Well," I say, "the first rule of success, Michael, is to never have an opinion. We're bright young men. Tweed is not a bright young man. He's old and married. He told me once you either get married young and cheat on your wife for ten years, or you don't get married and cheat for ten years. You see what I mean?"

"Why not just wait till you fall in love?" Michael wonders.

"Well, I don't know. Tweed is a broken personality, man, standardized. His family has been in this country for generations. He exaggerates nothing, not even his handicap. And he was in the Navy, so he only hears what he's already heard. Americans who have survived the military have an entirely different set of emotions than Americans like you and me. So if you find yourself trying to think differently—*What if I don't want to kill the enemy?*—you're out of line, disobeying orders. When Spreckman tells you his strategy, and asks for your opinion, all you ever say,

ever, are these seven words: *Yes, I'm guessing that may be true.*
Believe me, he's saying it to the guy above him. Let him know you
know your place. Be a slave. That'll make you a free man."

"I'm guessing that may be true," Michael says.

"See. You can do it."

"Does KK say that?"

"No, Krista has her own language. She uses 'consternation' a
lot."

"Well, she's a rising star."

"Yeah she's a rock star."

"She is. She's a top performer, coach. I'll never be like that."

"But you can't think that, Michael. You have to act as though
you're the top performer, too. You know? Act as if you are a free
man."

"What's being a free man going to do for me?" After he asks
his questions, Michael's light brown eyes look up at me. I'm the first
man Michael's ever met who teaches him anything about the real
world. I get used to it. I like having an audience, even an audience
of one. I enjoy waltzing over to the pulpit he builds for my
speeches.

"Well, for one thing, free men get paid. And you'll get fed
better food. Tweed will start asking when you and him are going to
grab that steak."

O

After that magical week when I went over to her place every
night, Krista and I stopped talking, which turned out to be a good
thing for helping me repair some things with Jenny. But now that
Krista and I are firing a black man together, we've been hanging

out more. Tweed charged her with staying close to me during Michael's termination, to make sure I don't go soft.

"This is an important career progression, Ty," she reminds me.

"Yeah but I'm no better than Michael."

"Of course you are."

"I once called him a slave. Or I said at work everyone's a slave. Do you think he's going to bring that up?"

"No," Krista says thoughtfully. "If he remembered to bring up something granular like that, he wouldn't be getting fired in the first place."

It really is all my fault. I only offered him the job because we both liked *Godfather III*. And because we were from the same Queens. Sort of. We went to the same Junior High School for a year, never ran into each other. Which is the same thing that happened with Jenny and I. Michael also had his gear stolen on the playground. He also went to Queens College but we hung out on opposite ends of the campus. It doesn't matter. We're old buddies. Every time he makes a mistake, I tell him he's cool, and he agrees, nervously, yeah I'm cool. But he never does pick up a sense of context in a business setting. He thinks business people are supposed to love each other.

That business people are in this because they want to be friends.

"Work doesn't love you back," I say. "It just takes and takes. No one is ever going to love you at work. You have to love yourself."

Michael has trouble with this concept. He keeps saying 'trouble' instead of 'issue' and 'sure thing' instead of 'will do.' He can't get into the habit of responding straight back to emails to acknowledge their receipt. He keeps talking sports when it's time to quit talking sports.

We have hour-long discussions on the Barry Bonds steroid controversy.

I think Bonds belongs in the Hall of Fame.

Look at what he did with the Pirates in the 80s, that was enough.

Michael doesn't think Bonds belongs in the Hall.

Not because of the steroids, but because he lied.

"You don't think it has anything to do with his skin color?" I finally ask.

"No. Mark McGwire's white and he's in the same jam."

"That's true."

"But," Michael says, "It *does* have to do with the fact Bonds is an asshole."

Michael keeps talking about Bonds with the partners more than he talks about work. The partners don't care. They inform Tweed there's cause for concern. One even pulls me aside, I receive thoughtful notes. They understand the vagaries of hiring, and they stand behind the firm's diversity initiative, and they welcome all of these new perspectives, but they don't feel Michael Mann is pulling his weight. He can't get words out of his mouth unless they're unnecessary words. Not "like" or "I mean" but words like "when" and "if" out of nowhere, or closing a sentence with "there" when no direction is indicated.

"Are you remembering to say *I'm guessing that may be true*?" I ask him.

"I try, coach. It's hard."

"It is hard. That's why it's so valuable to do it."

O

"Money is not the most important thing to me," Michael told me during his interview. I rose out of my seat ready to hoist this large black man over my shoulders and deposit him out the inoperable window. His accelerated mass would flatten protestors, their cops, dozens of tourists from the American interior.

"I'd be happy to take your first paycheck off your hands," I said.

"What I meant," he recovered, "is that I want to belong to a team that values me. A team that values me for who I am."

"Right. Did you read that on the internet? I understand."

"I want work to change me," Michael said.

"A lifespan is too brief a time period for a man to change."

"Yes, sir."

"Listen, we're business intellectuals here. We're not stockbrokers rubbing money on our body, we're not going to strip clubs after work, we're not Dick Cheney, we're not Patrick Bateman, we're consultants. Consultants are the intellectuals of the business community. That's why everyone hates us. Do you know what an intellectual is?"

"Yeah, of, course."

"My girlfriend. She's a writer."

"What's she written?"

"Practically nothing. But she thinks she's an intellectual. She's not. She thinks she's not causing anyone harm. She is. You and I are the intellectuals, not her. You and I are Stalin. Do you know who Stalin was?"

"Yeah, from Russia."

"That's right. The Soviet Union. He wanted to be friends with intellectuals, because he was from a place like Queens and he wanted to get out and move to the big bad city. We're from Queens. We're like Stalin, or Lenin, whatever. We're intellectuals. Does that make sense?"

"Yeah, definitely," Michael said. "That sounds really exciting."

"Great. I have one more question. What do you think your favorite movie will be in five years?"

"What do you mean?"

"Tell me what you think about three or four time a day, and you don't really know why, and then you think about the same thing before going to bed. Basically, Michael, tell me a secret."

He sneezed. He knew his secret. He leaned over the table and began in a calm voice, with none of his unnecessary words: "So I have this theory. There are thirty-five, at least thirty-five, maybe one-hundred-and-thirty-five, Bobby D. movies that are lost."

"Bobby D.?"

"Robert De Niro. The best actor."

"Of course," I said.

"You kind of look like a young Bobby D.," Michael said.

"Thanks."

"You're Italian, right?"

"Basically. I'm Ashkenphardic-Sicilian."

"Got it. So between the time he made *The Godfather* and *Taxi Driver*, 1974 to 1976, there are actually no movies over that period. I have this theory. We don't know these movies exist yet. They're lost. Some of them are good, some are bad, but the point is they're Bobby D. movies. He's in them. And there are like two hundred of them."

I tapped my pen against the table.

"And I don't know what any of them are about, sir, but I know they're out there. And that keeps me up at night. That, sir, is my secret."

"Do you like *Godfather III*, Michael?"

"It's my favorite one."

"Perfect. But I lied. I actually have one more question. How do you feel about ambiguity?"

"I'm not sure, sir. It depends on the situation."

"Wonderful. I think you have a bright future with us. And Michael, feel free to call me coach."

○

Tweed calendars a quick status meeting. Krista and I walk down the hall past the imitation Rothkos. We know the decision has already been made to fire Michael and this is just a formality, a way to make Krista and I feel like we're part of the process. I cradle my Cambridge Stationers notebook, my hanging files. Krista is hands free. The scent of her wild strawberry perfume follows us down the hall.

"We're beyond blame," she says. "You know this is the beginning of the end."

"No, I don't think that's true. Not if we stand up for him."

"What does that mean, *stand up for him*? This isn't a scene from *School Ties*."

"Right."

"When Brendan Fraser is black at the prep school."

"Yeah, I know the film."

"And no one *stands up for him*, remember?"

"You've made your point, Kaplan, you don't see color."

"This isn't about him being African-American," Krista says.

"I know that. You're right."

She wears a navy pantsuit, the spikes of her snakeskin heels muffled by the corridor carpet. Her hair is combed back so tight I wonder if it's hurting her brain. The hairstyle is an advertisement for combs.

"Come shopping with me after this," she says.

"Century 21?"

She slows me down, holds my hand against her white blouse. We hear footsteps around the corner and cut it out.

"Century 36DD, you mean. I don't know."

"I'm making a move," she says.

"I mean, I don't know what's going on with Michael."

"He's being separated from the firm."

Tweed waves us into his office. He's wearing a black suit, not his usual navy blazer. His hair is also parted on a different side.

"I can appreciate that," he says, before hanging up the phone. "You guys mind if I spit?"

"Spit your heart out," Krista says.

We sit down. Spreckman retrieves a dented Styrofoam cup and pouch of tobacco from his desk drawer. He pinches up a plug of tobacco and sockets the round nug in the lower part of his mouth. He chews, chanks, heaves, spits into the cup. His face turns an even brighter shade of red.

"Why the black suit?" I ask.

"Funeral this morning."

"Sorry to hear that," I say. As a Navy veteran, Tweed attends dozens of early morning funerals.

"Tweed I *love* your office," Krista says. "I know I've told you this before."

Tweed is forced to share an office with an individual called the Head of New Design. We never see this Head outside of monthly meetings when he updates us, via conference call from Los Angeles or Stockholm, on the emerging trends in his field.

"Thank you, Kaplan," Tweed says. "I'll pass it on to the faggot. Sorry if faggot is inappropriate. I take that back if it offends you."

"Faggot is fine," Krista says. She looks up at the painting on the wall. "Tenuous to have a nude individual in a picture, don't you think?"

Most offices in the building are decorated in a traditional manner. There are Rothko prints, baseball pennants, Twombly scribbles, framed photos of soccer youths, bursts of abstract expressionist energy, cystic fibrosis charity dinner salt and pepper shakers. But Tweed's shared office is different. It makes a design statement, admits the better things in life. There are boldly colored files and folders, pink mobiles hanging from the ceiling, non-charity-dinner iridium paperweights, framed postcards of scalloped bays, exotic flowering plants, a solar-powered banker's lamp, a noiseless desk fan, and a framed Balthus print which Krista and I both recognize from the Met, *Nude Before a Mirror.*

We all look up at this painting. The nude is on the plump, mature side for Balthus. She stands in a wallpapered room in front of a fireplace. There seem to be holes in the wallpaper, possibly peepholes: horny butlers and frustrated cooks are spying on the nude just like we are. Above the fireplace, on the mantel, sits a blue water pitcher the color of a purple ghost, and an angled mirror. The nude stands directly in front of that mirror, a cataract of brown hair, hip-hop dancer extensions, flowing down her otherwise hairless body. She runs her hands through, holds a makeshift ponytail. Even though her eyes appear to be closed she smiles, pleased by whatever it is she sees in the mirror, or whatever she's thinking in her head. She just can't help checking herself out. Her competition is fierce, and in no rush to turn in their tiaras, but this nude may be the most stuck-up woman to ever appear in a picture. And there's no doubt a naked 1950s teen hanging on the walls of a shared office is just absurd, inappropriate, and possibly deleterious to the person's career who hung it up. Any nude of any era, from any age or any gender—even a chubby horn-blowing angel, a British orphan with no knickers, a smooth shepherd-in-training, lazy bathers, anyone anywhere near a toilet—might cause offense without meaning to, which is still sexual harassment. That's why there are Rothkos in every pot, and that's one of the reasons, in many of my moods, I find abstraction offensive.

"He's a pedophile," Tweed gurgles through his tobacco.

"What do you mean?" Krista asks.

"He molests little kids."

Tweed spits tobacco into his cup. I lean over in my seat to steal a glance at the backwash, it ruins my attention, the color of split bark after a rainstorm.

"Who's a pedophile, the Head of New Design?" I ask.

"That's horrible," Krista says.

"No this painter. Balthasar Klossowski." Tweed enunciates the name like he's reading it off the business card of a Goldman head of ops. "A Polish count. He painted little girls, so what else could he be? Definitely a pedophile. It's like that song."

"Which song?" Krista asks.

"Frankie Valli. 'My Eyes Adored You.' But the man in that song never laid hands. You know this Polish count didn't just adore with eyes. He *laid hands*."

"Did you hear that," Krista says to me, "he laid hands."

"That's right, Kaplan. He laid hands. Now. Why are we having this meeting?"

"Michael Mann," I say.

"Yes. He's in his probationary period, which makes this less onerous, considering how onerous it's been anyway."

"It's certainly presented me with unnecessary consternation," Krista says.

"Listen," I say, "maybe we're getting ahead of ourselves. I think Michael can improve."

"Would you stake *your* career on that? It's not like we don't have enough work to do on top of the work he does wrong," she says. Then: "I'm tired of this, Tweed."

"No one knows that more than me," I say. "I pick up most of Michael's work, not you, Krista. But I still believe Michael can improve. I think he can figure it out. He's confided in me, and he's dealing with a lot of problems on the home front. Real problems. Not like I believe any of us are dealing with."

Krista and Tweed both look at me, waiting for me to disclose Michael's personal problems.

"I'd rather not delve into his personal problems in this setting," I finally say.

"But why don't you?" Tweed says. "Regardless of what you'd rather do."

"Okay. He talks about killing himself."

"No one kills themselves because they lose their job."

"Yeah but if he loses this job…"

"He just graduated college," Krista says. "Are we even certain of that? Did we verify his transcripts?"

"Don't you think that's a little racist," I say.

"Excuse me?"

"If he were a white man, would you ask if we verified his transcripts?"

"This has nothing to do with race," Krista says. "I never bring it up, only you do."

"This is not about color," Tweed says. "We don't see color."

"Losing this job," Krista says, "which he's not cut out for, will be the best thing that ever happened to him."

"She's right," Tweed says. "He's not a good fit here. He seems to be comprehensively preoccupied with other things. "He seems almost..." and Tweed Spreckman sounds like he's going to puke when he says this word... "*dreamy*. We can't allow his kind of dreams here. We *can* release him during this probationary period and he will leave thinking it was the least onerous thing for both parties."

"Which it will be," Krista adds.

"Whatever you guys think," I say.

"You need to be there to walk him out of the final meeting," Tweed says to me.

"Can't you be involved?" I ask.

"Wish I could. Client commitments."

"What about you?" I ask Krista.

"She's got the same client commitments."

Krista and I stand up. She leaves the office. Tweed asks me to stay behind for a second.

"One thing."

"Yeah, anything," I say. And I would do anything. The thought of firing someone makes me terrified to lose my own job.

"You remember when I got you into this, and I told you hiring is a personal process? Well, separation is just like that, but it's an impersonal process."

"That makes sense."

"I'm glad to hear you say that. This individual…"

"Michael Mann…"

"…this individual is just a number on a spreadsheet now. He has no value to us and we have no value to him. Once it's over, and you walk him downstairs, you just walk to the door. You don't say his name. You don't go back outside with him. You don't walk him up the street. You just let him go."

"Let him go," I nod.

"Yes," Tweed says. "Let him go. And don't forget to shave tomorrow, Tyrone."

○

"That was real beautiful of you," I say to Krista in the hall. "To stick up for him like that."

"What do you mean, *stick up for him*? This isn't *School Ties*…."

"I know, I know."

"Let's stop by my desk. I need the thing."

"For what?"

"Century 36DD. Where is it?"

My heart stops, thinking our journey into a world of exclusive women may not happen because of a coupon.

"Found it," she smiles, showing me a pink card. "You sure you're not busy?"

"I've got nothing better to do," I say.

"You'll be my suit consultant, then. What are your rates?"

"You can't afford me," I say, but I feel bought and sold.

O

We ride the elevator downstairs.

Krista hails a taxi.

Two stop.

We head uptown.

"I guess firing someone is the exact same process as hiring someone," I think out loud. "It's just the other way around. You never want them more than when you hire them. You never want them less than when you fire them."

"You know how to dump people. Are you seeing anyone?"

"You say that like I'm cheating on you."

"Do you have a girlfriend?"

"Don't get so personal."

"Scooch over."

I hold her hands to my mouth. In the taxi her perfume is no longer wild strawberry, more high-fructose breakfast pastry. Her fingernails are painted a dark purple and she wears a purple gemstone ring I never see again.

O

The boutique is on the edge of SoHo, up a flight of stairs. We are buzzed in. The salesgirl leads us down a narrow curtained hallway to another room partitioned by curtains. In that room there is a fitting room behind another curtain, a small table and one leather armchair. I sit in it. There are free-standing merchandise racks behind me stocked with cover-ups.

I learn the word shift, I learn the word *pāreu*.

Krista and the salesgirl discuss options. The salesgirl confirms Krista's measurements and says she'll be right back.

"Did they really need a whole store for this?"

"Who are they?" Krista asks.

"Women. Your people."

"This store isn't for all women, puppy. I want to give them a chance. They're really persistent."

The salesgirl, who I can now see is also plus-sized, returns with two bikinis. Krista takes them and walks through the dressing room curtain. I sit down, sip a Smeraldina and flip through a book on the table called *ESCAPES*.

"Where do you plan on swimming?" I ask, walking toward her curtain.

"For Hanukkah. My Dad and I are going to St. Kitts."

I don't know where that is.

"Do you want to see white or orange first?" Krista says.

"Orange."

I tug on the curtain.

"It's really creamsicle."

We are two young businesspersons who will combine our salaries and one day, with the help of Krista's father, purchase a large two-bedroom condo in East Midtown, with a view of both Citi towers, Manhattan and Queens. Our children will grow up as culturally aware New Yorkers, liberals, fashionably guilty, fair; they will attend strong colleges, maybe even Oberlin or Brown University. For them there will be no streets left. Their entire life will be the management of high quality. They will play soccer at rush hour in the middle of Third Avenue as flying taxis honk overhead. Our family will be a spackle of frosting licked from the vanilla fingers of Manhattan, serviced by professionals that have our pleasure and comfort in mind, protected by police who draw their guns in the other direction.

"So I'm about to take this suit off. Do you want to consult?"

"Well, that's what I'm here for."

Krista parts the curtain, wearing the creamsicle bikini top. A silver stud fills her small belly-button, defines the brown cuts in the smooth muscles surrounding it. She is still wearing her navy suit pants, though, and snakeskin heels.

"Where's the bottoms?"

"My bottom is normal."

"Not really."

"How does it look? You're my consultant and I'm paying for your time. Give me a deliverable."

"Well," I consult, "things could go either way depending on several other factors outside of the scope of this project, but the suit has a deep understanding of your needs. It hugs your body with the fit you require. It meets or exceeds all of your tan lines, beyond your expectations. It looks like it should be slutty but it's not slutty. But maybe that's you, not the bathing suit."

"That's what you pay for."

I move closer and drop my mouth to her shoulder. I try to make my lips as small as the lone freckle on the near slope. I open my eyes, stare into hers. I feel beautiful in the wrong place, like a sidewalk flower. She gives me her tongue. I let her get away.

She pushes me outside the dressing room and goes back behind the curtain. "What's your advice," she says, her voice wavering in and out, like speakerphone, "on my Omaha meeting tomorrow?"

"Your client commitments. Are you flying to Omaha?"

"No the meeting is in Midtown. Question: Should I wear my hair up or down?"

"You don't need my advice on how to wear your hair. You know what to do."

I need to let myself out of my pants. I unbuckle my belt, my pants, unclasp the button on the inside, pull them down as little as possible to relieve some of the tension. Whenever I'm around Krista, it's the biggest it's ever been. And when I look down the narrow hallway leading to the front of the store, I see the salesgirl laughing at me. I hop to the left, out of her line of sight.

"Wear it up. Pulled back. Like now. Have you been to St. Kitts before? Wear it exactly the way it is today."

"That's what Tweed said, too. Pull it back. He said I look like a scalped Seminole. If I had a problem with scalped in reference to Native Americans, though, he takes that back."

"He is such a creep. Such a creep. I swear, the biggest creeps are our nation's heroes."

"He's harmless. And we're all creeps."

"You think saying we're all creeps gives us all permission to be creeps. You think it takes Michael's blood off your hands."

"Money is the only thing in my hands," Krista says. "Okay, ready."

I step across the threshold, my pants down, my palms trying to cover myself until I give up. Once again, Krista isn't wearing the suit bottom, but this time her pants are off. I hoist her up on the modular ledge, move her panties to the side. They are a darker shade of white than the bikini top.

"Do you have your period?"

"No it's over."

"I don't know."

The sands of St. Kitts. The heave of white tennis mornings. Long nights, lush and stormy. Tomorrow's sun our only commitment.

Michael worries that all we do is help companies ruin the world. That's not true, I tell him, we help companies become more efficient. I read that, I tell him, in an article on *Yahoo!* Finance. And we've got the efficiency numbers to prove it. You can't survive otherwise. It sounds like the oldest trick in the world, but you need to learn to play the game. Everyone nowadays thinks they control the game. No. You're still playing it. You need to look only to the next play, with blinders on. Like we're helping Goldman Sachs with just this one thing. We're not the reason Goldman is the devil. Do I believe that? What does it matter. Goldman's socio-cultural reputation is managed by Goldman's charitable giving and corporate responsibility arm. Not our arms. Unless we're working on a particular project involving those arms. Whatever arm we're washing, we're washing *just this one thing.* We need to evacuate the rest out of our minds, scrape the plaque of objections off the organizational heart. If you can't achieve that level of exclusion and concentration, if you can't zero in on *just this one thing*, then maybe our job isn't for you. Maybe it's not for me, Michael tells me. I feel like a slave sometimes, he says. Well, you are a slave. Why did I say that! Welcome to the world of management consulting. Welcome to the world of gazing on the crooked skyline and seeing nothing but your client's next request. Serious word to use, slave. Historical baggage comes with throwing that word around. I'm quoting an article I read on *Yahoo!* Sports.

"Don't stop, don't stop, come in me," Krista says. I come and then I pull out, hold my fingers inside her, bring some come up to her mouth, a few of my hairs, her blood. We kiss, I'm warmer than a hot wheel, some of my come ends up on my lips.

"*Shayna punim*," Krista says.

She purchases both bathing suits, and another one, basic black, which she doesn't try on. She pays with a dark American Express and I catch what must be her father's first name on the raised gold lettering.

"Come again," the sales girl smiles at us.

O

Krista hails a taxi.

Two stop.

She smells them both and sends them away.

She hails another.

The next two both smell good and I get to pick.

"If you're not doing anything you should try and come."

"I just did," I say, and the clothing around my groin—shirt, the perforated bottom of my undershirt, the waistband of my slacks, the elastic band of my briefs—are all stuck together. "But come where?"

"St. Kitts. Look for last-minute deals."

"That would be a move, if I came with you and your Dad to St. Kitts."

"I don't know if you're capable of that move."

"I'll look for last-minute deals."

When we get back to the office, Krista will have the energy to get right back to work and prepare for tomorrow's client commitments. I will look up St. Kitts and learn it's an island in the British Caribbean. Under-touristed, a big murder-rate where tourists don't go, it has a dormant volcano the natives call Mt. Misery. But I will also need to walk Michael to the door when he gets fired.

"Scooch over. Remember, you don't have to stop being yourself when you're with me. Be yourself, just let me in on it."

"Right. You've mentioned that. Let you in on it. Got it."

"I don't really care about your girlfriend."

"I know," I say. "I wish you did."

○

I don't take Tweed's advice.

When it's over, I follow Michael Mann out of the building.

"You called me featherbrained once, coach," he cries, undoing the foil on a pack of Marlboro Menthols. He is adding his nonsense words, "here" and "if"—I wonder why he does that, when his weird problem started and if he even notices it, what it means for him, why he never tried to clean it up.

I'm drained, physically tired, emotionally numb. Michael is the opposite of drained—he's filled with sadness, shocked by the rejection. I don't believe him when he says he didn't see it coming. He starts crying and he's the first black man I've seen cry since the playground. At least in real life. I watch black people crying on the local news all the time.

"I'm sorry if I called you featherbrained."

"*If* you called me featherbrained? You did call me featherbrained. My sister said that's a racist thing to say. I didn't even know that."

"I'm sorry," I say, fighting back a yawn.

"Don't let me keep you up, coach."

"Sorry. It's because of the cold. And what difference does it make what I think? You're not featherbrained, Michael. You're not featherbrained."

"You said I am, coach," he cries. "You think I'm Woodstock on top of Snoopy's house."

"That's ridiculous. Who cares what I think, what's the difference?"

"It makes a difference. I told my sister I look up to you."

"Come on. I mean, think of De Niro. He would act his way out of anything, right? Bobby D., right? He probably got fired all the time before he became a star."

"Bobby D.," Michael says, coughing on his cigarette.

"Always. Give me one of those. You're going to be fine."

"I'm going to kill myself," he says, lighting my cigarette.

"Don't say that. You're not going to kill yourself. Nobody has ever killed themselves after lighting a friend's cigarette."

"You're not my friend. I mean, I'm sorry, I thought you were, but..." Michael cries. "I'm sorry. You must be so disappointed in me."

"No, of course not. It just wasn't a good fit for you here. It was onerous on all of us."

"Just ignore me. I know that's not fair. I know it's not your fault. I don't know what I'm saying."

"You're going to find another job. This will turn out to be a good thing," I say, swallowing the smoke and my persistent yawn. "Let me tell you a story."

"I do like your stories, coach."

"Here's one. So I'm at my cousin's wedding, right, and my Dad, he does the reading, you know, from Corinthians. So everyone in my family is constantly crying at weddings, right, they can't get over themselves, but not my Dad. And he helped my mom..."

"What happened to your mom?"

"She had breast cancer."

"I'm sorry. Where did you and Krista go, did you guys have a meeting in Midtown?"

"Yeah. For Omaha."

"I won't get to work on Omaha now!" He starts crying again.

"It's okay. Omaha will survive you. So my Dad, he can do it, right, for some reason. He's strong, my Dad. Which is weird because he's a sentimental guy at other times and weak in totally ever other way. He never leaves the house, just watches *Superman* and *Rocky* all day."

"Sounds like a great life," Michael says. "Although I would add *Clueless* to that."

"Something about weddings hardens all that. He says the old words without choking up, so he gets tapped for the bible readings. I don't usually listen, right, I mean, to anything my father says. But this wedding I was listening, for some reason, and he pronounced..."

"You're convulsing, coach," Michael says. "I've never seen you like this."

"Sorry. He goes....if I don't have love...if I don't have love...I am a resounding gong! I am a resounding gong! Do you know this bible thing? If I speak in the tongue of men or angels, but do not have love, I am only a resounding gong."

"It's charity, though. Right?"

"What is?"

"The bible is. You're a clanging cymbal if you don't have charity, not if you don't have love. At least that's what it is at our church."

"Yeah there are so many bible translations," I say quickly, although I am taken by Michael's distinction, and the word 'charity' does stick in my head.

"Sometimes I think you were lying to me," Michael says. "About how I was doing here. Like you knew this was going to happen, you knew I was going to get let go. That's not fair to you, I know. I know it's not fair to you to say that. I don't know what I'm saying."

"I didn't want to lie to you. What was your favorite subject in school?"

"Biology."

"Great. You should think about doing something in biology. What's an example of a career in biology?"

"Maybe I could work in a lab?"

"That's right, maybe you could work in a lab."

"What happened with Omaha when you and Krista were in Midtown?"

"Not much. You know what Nas says, the sexiest girls are always the nastiest."

"Did Nas say that? I didn't know Nas said that."

"You're from the Big Q and you don't even know your gospels."

"I do love it when you call Queens the Big Q, coach!"

"You're from the Big Q and I bet you don't even know that girl Ramelle."

"You know what? I don't. I don't know a girl named Ramelle."

"I have to get back upstairs."

We say goodbye. Michael is going home, dealing with the worst, but all I do is go through the revolving door, back to business, and I'm surprised at how easy I find it to move on to what's next.

O

Michael Mann does kill himself. At least that's what his sister thinks. According to the official story in the paper—page 4 of the *Post*, page 5 of the *News*, nothing in the *Times*—he's run down after midnight by the Q60 bus on Queens Boulevard, the Boulevard of Death, as the papers call it, where no pedestrian, however careful, is ever safe. But according to Heidi Mann, her brother stepped in front of that Q60.

She's sure of it.

"I'm calling you because he's gone, sir. He talked about you more than anyone else from the city."

"I'm glad you called," I say to Heidi, who has the clear, practical, nonpartisan voice of the bookish high school freshman. She doesn't cry, from what I can tell, the whole time we're on the phone. I don't either, but when we get off I'm filled with disbelief and tremendously sad.

They say the people who need to know, know.

I guess I'm one of the people who needed to know that Michael Mann died.

O

I ask Jenny to come with me to Michael's wake. I can't think of doing it in any other way. I need to delegate my public mourning to a woman.

"Why don't you take indescribable rack?"

"Stop it. Forget her. She doesn't even think she's obligated to go. Tweed doesn't think he's obligated to go, either."

"Tweed," Jenny says.

"Yeah. He doesn't think he needs to go, no one at work thinks they need to go."

"Work," Jenny says. "You're all a bunch of racist dipshits."

"We can't all sit at home footnoting our brave essays."

"Why can't we?"

"According to my co-workers, Michael was dead the day his name got added to a spreadsheet that kicked him off the payroll. When I told Tweed Michael was dead, the first thing he asked me was what charity to send money to in lieu of flowers."

"Lieu," Jenny says.

"I told you what Tweed said, right. To fire a black man, you must overwrite."

"To make a white man feel," Jenny says, "that firing a black man isn't about color, you must write so much you forget how to read."

"Just like my semen on your brave essay isn't about me, it's about you."

"I can't think of a worse way to go," Jenny says.

"Getting hit by a bus. What do you think it feels like?"

"Yeah. But specifically, the Q60. I mean I'd rather go by the B58, if it had to be a bus."

I must convince Jenny to tag along. I need her to figure out whatever it is I'm supposed to say to Michael's family. This is what

I want from a long-term relationship. A woman who will perform my mourning, flirt with my father, remember important dates, wrap the presents.

Now I hear the sizzle of kitchen shears across a ribbon, fashioning a curl.

"Come on, I'll stay by you the entire time."

"I'm no good at funerals."

"People die, though. Nobody is. And it's not even a funeral, it's a house party thing, you know, the wake."

"Call me after."

"I'm going to spend the entire time in the bathroom," I threaten.

"Don't go, then! You don't have to go."

"I feel like I have to. But I'm going to spend the entire time in the bathroom,"

"OK," Jenny says. "Don't forget to flush."

O

The Mann family requests immediate relatives only at the cemetery. Everyone else is welcomed to their apartment afterwards. They live in Kew Gardens. Their apartment faces the boulevard down which rides the bus that killed their son.

It's an old apartment building, forgotten by everyone except the people who live there, a fancy name above the entryway arch (The Excelsior), broken buzzers and an unlocked front door, a pane of glass missing right by the doorknob. The dark front hallway reeks of mice, mice-killing spray, and mice eliminations. The elevator has a rusted viewing window, diamond-shaped. I have to pull the elevator door open. The elevator ascends slowly, at the speed of climbing warped stairs.

I share the ride with a black woman dressed in black, but I don't assume she's headed to the same wake that I am.

The Mann family—pale, tired, furious. They're the first crying black family I've seen outside of a newscast, or the happy tears of my elementary school graduation. I think of the cover of Andrew Hill's album, *Grass Roots*, the white and black boy playing in the wood chips, but I don't think of it too much.

All of that's over.

I'm a white adult now.

Many family members aren't crying. Many seem stoic, understand this isn't the hard part, it's what comes after. All of them, though, look possessed.

If they didn't before, they certainly believe in the devil now.

As soon as chairs are unfolded, mourners rush to them. It reminds me of a game of musical chairs and I'm so far away when the music stops I'm for sure going to be eliminated. I'm told, though, that the chair in the middle has been reserved for me. And for a short time I sit in the center of family action and accept questions, tell sweet stories about Michael's progress at the firm, what a great job he did on his most recent project, how we, the firm, might even win this project because of his strategic contributions. Michael's relatives egg me on. They had no idea he was working on things for important companies like Goldman Sachs.

There's a moment of silence, only we don't call it that.

The topic changes to Michael's cultural interests.

The family knows that I too share a love for Robert De Niro, or Bobby D., as Michael called him. Michael and I had plans, according to Michael, to watch Bobby D. movies together, here, at his place. Such lies are repeated again and again: I was supposed to come over for dinner, Friday night Filet-O-Fish, and watch movies in his bedroom. I was also going to attend a baseball game with Michael and Heidi, at Shea or up at the Stadium. Heidi's initial comment to me on the phone is repeated, by Michael's mother and his father, and his grandmother, who is the first blind person of any race I ever see cry, that Michael talked about me, cared about me more than anyone else from the city.

From the city comes out of everyone's mouth and I get the impression that this Queens family goes into Manhattan only to see Fifth Avenue at Christmas. They look at Atlas holding up the world and think to themselves—hey, I relate to this guy, I'm holding up the world too and it's so heavy.

From the city is a character in their son's tragedy and contributed, according to their interpretation of events, to Michael's pointless, brutal death.

Boundlessly disgusted with myself for each and every one of my impressions and speech patterns and observations and for my undeserved, unearned elevated place during this family funeral, I excuse myself from the mini-circle of which I am the star member. I should be finding Heidi, but instead I step into the bathroom off the kitchen.

I plan on hiding in here for the rest of my life.

If only Jenny were in here with me.

On the bathroom wall there is a turn switch for a heat lamp that doesn't exist, a painted-over laundry chute, framed postcards of Renoir's bathers above the toilet. I piss like an old man, not much flow and it burns. I go to unroll some toilet paper to wipe my piss drops off the floor until I notice, below me, that someone, probably

Michael's mother, has already placed two floriated paper towels at the foot of the bowl, to absorb men, probably Michael's father, who piss poorly like I just did. Not Michael. He's dead. He will never experience the pleasures of pissing again.

I'm confused because now those towels are semi-damp with my droplets.

Should I replace those towels?

There's nothing I can do about it.

I'm not going to throw away those towels and go to the kitchen to find new ones to repave the foot of the bowl.

Behind the mirror, the medicine cabinet items are in mourning. Even though I have a headache, and could use some aspirin, I am so sure of their mourning that I'm scared to open the cabinet and disturb them. One day, when dying becomes a product, I look forward to consuming advertising creativity which will anthropomorphize an over-the-counter remedy's reaction to a sudden human death. The acetaminophen weeping, too weak from tears to use the choked-up swabs. Twofers of day and night cold medicine at such a loss for symptoms, they dose each other.

Perhaps dying is already a product, perhaps this ad is already out there.

When I get out of this place, I'll search for it online.

The gas heat stirs, crackling like an alien transmission. On the toilet top is a Yankee scorecard, each half-inning scored in two different handwritings. I recognize Michael's—blocky, shaky, indecisive about how to mark a stolen base—the other one clean, sharp, not erased, it has to be Heidi Mann's. Above the scorekeeping she wrote, "We're going for the sweep!" and then, below it, after the victory: "Bring out the brooms!"

I gulp to taste my breath. There's a new tube of Close Up on the sink ledge. But in the wastebasket, lined with a garbage bag for a larger canister, I notice an old tube of Whitening Crest with several squeezes left. It seems ridiculous to throw away an expensive tube of Crest paste in order to begin a Close Up so I tweeze the Crest tube out of the garbage and slab a brushful of gel, not paste, onto my finger. I am not a good finger-brusher and I end up swallowing enough of the paste to wonder if eating a finger of sodium laurel sulfate is harmful to the human body.

"Whose human body?" I think to myself.

"Yours," I answer, until I realize we're all here to mourn the absence of a body. It is bad luck in such situations to speak of your own. The absence of a body who didn't care about money but chose a job on Wall Street, the absence of a featherbrained mind who referenced Snoopy, *Clueless,* and truly believed, or told us all that he truly believed, there were 35, no, 135, lost Bobby D. movies made between '74 and '76. A black man who thought Bonds didn't deserve to be in the Hall, a black man who thought Spike should cool it with the catcalls at the Garden.

When I finally open the bathroom door, Heidi's standing in front of it.

Even standing right in front of me, Heidi Mann seems out of reach.

"I thought you fell in."

"Heidi. I knew that was you in the elevator."

"Why didn't you say hello?"

"Why didn't you?"

"I did, but you didn't hear me. I like your skinny tie."

"Thanks."

"If Michael were here he'd show you his room. I'll take you there."

When we worked together Michael and I spent coffee break time discussing how we could get him to move to Manhattan, or at least Astoria. Nothing in his childhood bedroom, however, suggests that he wanted to get out of Kew Gardens. Or that his childhood was over.

The room looks *lived-in*. The *Post* from the day before he died sits on his night table, opened to the crossword puzzle which he'd half-finished. Next to the *Post* there is a one-of-a-series baseball-themed mystery novels, *The Case of the Stolen Equipment*. On the walls there are posters of De Niro in *Goodfellas*, *Taxi Driver* and *Godfather II*, and of Nas, Public Enemy, KRS-One, EPMD; Yankee posters and cut-outs and baseball cards arranged in unique patterns, and the Kurt Cobain *SPIN* magazine cover where Cobain wears sunglasses, a green sweater with green and yellow trim, purple hair.

"Come on over and shoot the shit," I say to Heidi.

"That's what we're all here for," she answers.

"Michael pretended he didn't know Nas lyrics. All the words past the margin."

"He didn't," Heidi says. "A lot of these posters were our cousin's. But that one is Michael's," Heidi says, pointing to a poster of Snoopy lazing atop his doghouse, Woodstock circling above him.

"And the *Clueless* poster, right."

"Yeah. I'm taking that one."

"You should. Michael thought I thought he was featherbrained. I said that once and I want to apologize to you."

"You don't have to apologize to me," Heidi says.

"But I want to."

At the side of Michael's mother-made bed is a biography of Joseph Stalin and stacks of classic board games and deluxe card games, more than I've ever seen in another man's room—Michael still had all the varieties of Uno every 11-year old wants, none of which are as good as the normal Uno. I see some materials from our workplace, too, and even the graph he used to plot his personality during group orientation.

I pick it up to see the results.

Michael had the personality of a COLLEAGUE.

His key words: friendly, extroverted, easy-going.

20,000 colleagues under the sea.

"Where are his biology books?" I ask Heidi.

"What do you mean?"

"I thought they'd be here. Michael was good at bio."

"Really?"

Those were going to be his next steps after being fired. And I would've helped him during the job search. It would've been the right career path for a man who doesn't like money, to leave management consulting and explore a career in the field of biology, perhaps as a lab tech, a researcher or even pre-med. Michael could have been a hospice nurse. No matter how much he suffered taking care of the dead, he would have known that the dying suffer more. Before he was dead himself, this was Michael's path. He said to me: *I want people to value me for the person I am.* The impossible dream. If he lived, he'd work in bio, work in a hospice, and he wouldn't feel like a slave anymore.

"I called your brother a slave once. I can't believe I did that."

"He told me he felt like a slave sometimes," Heidi says. "But you talked him through it."

"Yeah, I talked him through it. That's what I do."

"It sounds so dark," Heidi says. "Why would anyone want to be a slave, just for money."

On his dresser a box TV with bunny ear antennae, built-in VCR, videotape covers for rundowns of Yankee championship seasons, also the one tape with a rundown of the Mets championship season. I pick up a seemingly basic key chain, it has a small speaker with a red button. I press the button. It's the voice of Knicks announcer Mike Walczewski introducing Patrick Ewing, his voice bridging the "trick" in Patrick to sit firmly on both sides of the full name.

"Isn't that cool?" Heidi says.

"Yeah very cool."

Michael's clothes are in a short boyhood dresser. The closet door is open and I can see Michael's work shirts and the suit he wore to his interview. Most of the closet is filled with women's dresses. Heidi and her mother use this closet for storage. I wonder if now they will force themselves, in honor of Michael, *not* to use it for storage. And outside of Michael's room he will still be dead and life will pile up.

I sit down on the sanctuary moon of the *Return of the Jedi* bedspread. I face the only window in the room. Heidi raises the blinds and sits down next to me. We look out onto the boulevard that killed Michael. It's eerily quiet.

"Now do this," Heidi says. "Look at the window. Look closely. Do you see him in the window? This is where I've been seeing him. This is where I think he is. Do you see him?"

"I don't know," I say.

"Just keep crying and it'll happen."

There are two types of crying when mourning the dead. The first, the simpler, is with your head down. This is crying for yourself. The second, much more difficult, is when you weep so hard you must raise your head and your neck juts forward. That's when you're crying not for yourself but for those who are gone. This is when you see them. Those tears are hydration for fantastic visions.

After what feels like a long while of working myself up—and once I start searching myself sadness isn't so hard to find—I finally do see Michael Mann, in a mirror of his window. He is hanging out there. In a Herman Miller swivel chair. He went shopping after death and he wears a black cashmere sweater, a starched white shirt with a spread European collar, dark wool pants, cinnamon brown oxford lace-ups, a wristwatch with Roman numerals. He holds a fountain pen in his hand. His short dreads are the dreads of the rappers from his cousin's posters on his bedroom wall.

He says, "Hey, coach, thanks for coming."

"What's up," I smile. "Of course."

I'm still holding the key chain in my hand and I press the red button so he can hear Ewing's name.

"I miss that," he says, as he mimics Walczewski's elaborations. Then Michael says, "I knew you were the only person who would come from the city."

"What are you writing?" I ask.

"There's a status meeting up here in heaven. I'm taking notes."

"Don't ask anyone to repeat anything," I say. "Just email them afterwards to close gaps."

I look over at Heidi. She's smiling, like me, but the Michael she's seeing isn't mine.

I tell Michael that I feel like it's maybe my fault he's dead. The room spins in a way that makes me feel less dizzy. Crying makes me feel like I'm not crying.

"It's the Q60, not you."

"I hate that fucking bus. I wish you got hit by the 58 instead of the 60."

"Come on. You taught me a lot, coach. I loved being alive when I was with you. Now I'm dead. It's always a long time coming, you know."

"I guess."

"You look like a young Bobby D."

"You think all Italians look alike, don't you. If we're pretty we look like DeNiro or Pacino and if we're ugly we look like Mario or Luigi."

"That makes so much sense, coach."

"From one of the lost movies," I say. "Have you found any?"

"Not yet. But I'm convinced they're around here somewhere. Like thirty-five. More like two hundred lost movies. And in each one of them Bobby D. says *no, I'm sorry, no, I'm sorry, but that's impossible.*"

"Yeah like 325 of them. Find them. Watch them. Watch them all. And I don't think you're featherbrained," I say, and it must be the first thing I say out loud because Michael disappears and Heidi asks me to stop saying that word.

"I'm sorry," I say. "Even though you said I don't need to apologize, I'm sorry. I need to explain to you why I'm saying it. I'm saying it because Michael thought he was Woodstock, on top of the dog house."

"Do you want to take the Knicks key chain as a memory?" she asks.

I look down at it in my sweaty hand. "No, you keep it."

"Take something."

"It's okay," I say. "I have enough. I need to get back to the city."

I follow Heidi out of Michael's room. It's colder in the living room, even though there are more people. Heidi says she will see me out. Michael's father stands up, and asks me to stay behind for a moment. I sense he wants me to hug him before I leave, so I do.

He talks and I focus on his white eyebrows, not his mouth.

I tell him again how sorry I am for his loss.

"Michael loved you, Tyrone. He talked about you more than anyone else from the city."

"I'm guessing that may be true."

"It's true, right Heidi?"

Heidi nods.

"There's no doubt about it," Michael's father confirms.

"I loved him too. I do love him. He lives on in our memory. I want to tell you, if there's ever anything you need from me, you should call me."

I hand him my business card. He holds it like it's the first business card he's ever seen. Then he hands me a baby-blue journal. "Did you sign this, coach? A remembrance book for Michael. Write down whatever you guys shared."

I turn to a page already cluttered with notes. I get my pen out of my jacket pocket and in a self-made corner I write the name: Bobby D.

O

Heidi walks me to the elevator.

"Getting warmer out there," I say as we go down. "Baseball season soon."

"Maybe. It's a shame you had to wait util Michael was dead to come over."

When we reach the lobby I try to let Heidi out first, but I realize she's going right back up. I hold the door so I can keep talking to her.

"Where do you guys go to church?"

"Here. In Jamaica."

"Cool. How do you get there?"

"We take the F."

"Cool. You know, I told Michael, you know, about this passage my Dad reads at weddings, the resounding gong. Do you know it? If you speak in the tongue of men or angels, no matter how eloquent you are, but you don't have love, you are only a resounding gong."

"It's charity, right?" Heidi says.

"Yes! That's what Michael said, too. I was wondering if you'd say it. I guess, I don't know. I guess I never associate charity with love. I associate charity with tax deductions."

"There's so many different translations," Heidi says.

"I know! That's what I think. So maybe we can hang out again. Maybe we can go to a Yankee game when the season starts."

"Maybe."

"In April, yeah, let's go."

I push my body against the elevator door and reach into my wallet to get a business card. "Your Dad has it, too. Opening day. My treat. We'll go to Shea, maybe the Bronx."

"Maybe."

"We'll get box seats. I can get great seats through the firm. Especially in April."

"I don't like sitting too close," Heidi says. "I'm scared of the ball."

"Really? I mean, I know what you mean. You don't strike me as someone who's scared of the ball. I hope you start feeling a little better."

"I feel a little better today."

"Do you like first base line or third base line? I love that spot between first and the plate. Let's think about it."

"Maybe. Take care, Tyrone."

"Heidi if you want to, you can call me coach. That's what Michael called me."

"I don't think you're my coach," Heidi says. "I think you're my nightmare."

"I don't know if I understand how to be friends with someone," I say.

"Nobody does. You just keep listening."

○

Before I go down to the subway I stop at the drugstore and buy a notebook. I choose the color baby-blue, like in Michael's remembrance book. In this baby-blue notebook I will record all of the conclusions I'll reach once I begin researching the differences and similarities between charity and love, between giving and withholding, between banishment and belonging. A drugstore single-ruled tablet where I'll ask questions and study pity in the sawed-off language. I find myself consumed by this idea about not having love, and not having charity, and how these two things are related and not related to being a resounding gong.

What is it that the gong does?

Makes noise.

Chatters teeth.

Keeps the unionized percussionist woke.

I go back home and realize that I too sleep in my childhood room. But I don't live in it the way Michael did, and I am dying to get out, I promise. How I love this room, hate this room, beat this room, lost to this room, won the doorstop war it waged against me. Childhood is no revolution. I sit in my room, clean my room, rearrange my room, hate my room, I have no patience for arrangements, no patience for concordance. The wonders of my room, my records, my instruments, my books, my posters and clippings, they are merely things, gigabytes of decay.

From my twin-sized bed I see my supermarket encyclopedias, v.17—MARIN-MONAD—still lost.

The Grateful Dead discovered their band name in Funk & Wagnalls but all I found was the capital of Zaire and confusion.

I bring all of my bibles to the bed and revisit the bible comparisons. Heidi and Michael were right. Sometimes, it's charity. But I am also right. Sometimes, it's love. Maybe it's not a question of right and wrong. The bible is always so much more complicated. There have to be volumes and volumes out there, great thinkers through the ages who tried to figure this out, and there's even a word in the original Greek, isn't there, which will complicate things even further.

I can bring an unlimited number of books to my twin-sized bed.

I've got a lot of work to do. And I promise myself I'll get to it.

Then I remember the sister Greta, who takes care of Gregor Samsa after he turns into a bug. She feeds him like a pet and waters him like a plant. "Why won't he eat?" Greta thinks. Because all Gregor wants is rotten cheese. Fresh meats and vegetables repulse him. So Greta gives the bug what it wants. And as Gregor devours the rotten cheese he knows very well it is a rotten thing to eat, he knows very well it is the rotten cheese which devours him. This realization makes Gregor cry *tears of contemplation*.

Those are the third kind of mourning tears—the sadness of being able to impartially judge your own actions from a meaningful distance.

I have choices. I choose to consume what's rotten. And the pleasure of latching on to garbage brings me here.

I don't deserve tears of contemplation.

If this is passage, I can't declare it.

What is there left to do? Never change? Shift weight from one foot to the other and make associations?

I don't think that's the answer.

Giving all, and having nothing.

Charity is what remains.

The Blindfold Faith

Lucky bridegroom!
Now the wedding you
Asked for is over

And your wife is the
Girl you asked for;
She's a bride who is

Charming to look at,
With eyes as soft as
Home, and a face

That love has lighted
With his own beauty.
Aphrodite has surely

Outdone herself in
Doing honor to you!
          —Sappho

Krista Kaplan co-leads the Omaha project. She travels to Omaha, and upon returning to New York tells me she didn't know ConAgra, the global food conglomerate, was based in Nebraska.

"What's the capital of Nebraska? Lincoln?"

"Um, it's ConAgra, puppy. ConAgra is the only thing in the entire state. Actually, I've been thinking all the state capitals are wrong. The real capital of a state should be its largest company."

I'm in the habit of thinking I love Krista Kaplan. When she says ConAgra, I hear something more like the name of a flower, *conagras*, native to the central plains.

Krista, my love, these are for you. They are conagras.

We enter conference rooms dedicated to fallen heroes. We form relationships. The partners think I'm the manager until I let them know Krista is my superior. My role is to speak when spoken to, ping people who are running late, erase implementation doodles from whiteboards. Krista writes the agenda, leads the discussion, enumerates key points, or she interjects. No one in the room, I sometimes think, knows what we've shared. But sleeping with the boss doesn't make you one. I am weakened by her lower lip, and her nose, never blown in public, her only feature modified by cosmetic surgery. The Reformed Temple of Bloomfield Hills Before and After Rhinoplasty Calendar. All proceeds help rebuild Detroit.

○

One Saturday morning, Jenny calls.

"Hey. Do you want to hang out?"

"Sure," I say.

"Are you sure you're not busy?"

"What's wrong?"

"Nothing. I'm just wondering if you're busy right now."

"Why are you wondering that? I don't like it when you wonder that. You know I am never busy when you call."

"Just wondering. No reason. Whatever."

"Where are you? You sound so far away."

"Brooklyn. Maybe come pick me up, if you're not doing anything? Go get my car. I'm near the bridge in a blue Celica."

I leave Dad and ride the B58 to Jenny's house, then I drive Big Red to the Brooklyn side of the Williamsburg Bridge. I'm extremely pissed to be in Brooklyn. I park Big Red right behind the blue Celica and I read a bumper sticker that says *Howl If You Love City Lights Books*. I don't howl. Instead, I sit on the horn. Jenny gets out of the Celica and I am still sitting on the horn. Man am I sitting on this horn. I don't take my arm off the horn until Jenny gets into the car and the guy in the Celica drives away. Only then do I think of getting the numbers on his Massachusetts license plate. I did catch a '7', but I can't make out if a letter is 'B' or 'D'.

What would that do, anyway? This is not a police procedural.

"You want to drive to the airport?" I ask.

"What for? No."

Jenny's hair is damp, her face paler than usual, there's a bruise below her eye, smeared Eleanor Rigby face kept in the jar by the door. Some of her hair is on her blazer. Why is she wearing a blazer? She smells like vomit. She brings one leg up and pulls off a penny loafer.

"You put actual pennies in your loafers? Who does that?"

"I don't know why I wore these," she says.

"Why are you wearing that blazer?"

"It has elbow patches."

The guy in the blue Celica is a creative writer, too, more an editor, the one who helped Jenny go deeper into her voice. According to his reading of Jenny's creative work—the essay where my jizz glosses the photograph—Jenny is into playing rough. And at first she is. She's definitely into telling me this story. But then the guy goes on. I can't get a clear answer on the exact length of time he goes on for. It sounds to me like porn. And if it were porn and Jenny were being compensated, this story would only be extreme. The compensation, in the editor's mind, is only delayed. When he stops, he claims he was trying to stop the entire time. All of the cocaine confused him. This is probably true, Jenny says, because all of it confused her too. Everything is really okay now. They decide to keep it between themselves and eventually they'll both get good material out of it, only Jenny's will be brave, whereas he will bury his impulses in overwrought fiction.

"Actually," I say, "you decided to not keep it between yourselves."

"What do you mean?"

"You told me."

○

I drive us back to my house. Dad is asleep, but we see Juan walking up the stairs with a Flying V in each hand. He invites us up to his place. We smoke a pin joint, listen to Obituary and Mayhem. Juan fills a water pipe. We take huge hits. I'm really stoned. Jenny can barely move and falls asleep.

I notice the irises I gave Juan are drooping in a different bong. I look around for the Schubert G-major album but give up trying to find it.

When we all wake up we're so stoned the only thing we can listen to is Sabbath. We smoke some more. This time I pass out, and when I wake up I see Juan trying to make out with Jenny, and she's letting him.

"Come on," I say to Jenny.

"You always know the next place to go, Ty."

"Time to go."

"Don't you want to finger me, Juan?"

"Let's go."

"Did you know that about Ty, Juan? He always knows where to go next. He knows all the cool spots in Midtown. He's such a hip meathead."

Downstairs, I make chicken strips and broccoli florets for everyone. We eat in front of the TV watching *Superman IV.*

Dad falls asleep. Jenny falls asleep. I fall asleep.

In the morning, everything's back to normal.

○

Jenny's new essay is giving her trouble. In her version of the event, she's an abused passenger being exchanged from a blue car to a red car, from one compact Japanese car to another, from the man who sort of physically abused her once (the editor) to the man who mentally abuses her day after day (me).

In the meantime, she publishes a poem titled "He Can't Even Brush His Teeth Unless a Woman is in Love With Him," an allusion to Michelangelo Antonioni's *Le Amiche*, which we watched one night after Richard Donner's *Superman II*. In bed that night, I'd said out of nowhere, there is a ghost on my toothbrush, the ghost of cavities past, and Jenny stole my line for her poem, which ended with her favorite word—balustrade. But Jenny is writing too much, she says, which is why she can't really finish anything. She's too dedicated to working, she says, which is why nothing gets done. More and more things don't get done. More and more things become too perfect to end. She read in Plath's journals that Plath promised herself to try this writing business long enough to see if she was any good at it. Jenny fears that she, Jenny, isn't any good at it. She's playing with language but it won't play fair. She's really down. She doesn't have writer's block, she says, more like writer's runs. Perfectionism harms her output. There are editors soliciting her work, only the barest crap needs to be given. Number any old list, call it *Thirteen Ways of Looking at My List*, and her editors will spin the list as brave. But she can't do it. Nothing will be clear, she says, to anyone but her.

"As long as I'm working. As long as I get something done for myself."

"Yeah but at what cost?" I say. "You need to move on."

"You think I should move to Brooklyn, don't you. You want me to leave my parents' house, Ty, but you never ask me to move with you to the city."

"Of course I don't want you to move to Brooklyn. But that's not really the idea, working for yourself. The idea is to work for others. Morton Feldman thought work was just getting something done every day, for himself, and he ended up composing eleven-hour pieces for string quartet."

I tell her one of Feldman's stories. He got a gig writing the score for a Hollywood feature. He had to write music for a rape scene near the climax of the film. During a storyboarding meeting, Feldman and the director discussed the rape's motivations and how to best supplement and enlarge the pathos of the scene with music. Feldman nodded. Sure, let's supplement the rape with massive orchestrations. But Feldman, being Feldman, didn't go that route. He wrote quiet, fragmentary rape scene music, stress-free, peaceful, elementary patterns. A lone viola bowing an open string. A muted celeste depressing one key. A haunting, evanescent, supreme point of view on sexual assault. And the director was furious. He said: She's being raped, and you write celeste music? She's being raped, and you give me a lone viola bowing an open string for six hours?

"What was it you wanted?" Feldman asked.

"I wanted something like *papa papa papa*," the director said.

"Papa, papa, papa?"

"Yeah. She's being raped for Christ's sake. I want something like papa papa papa. Give me papa papa papa. Give us papa papa papa papa papa papa."

O

I receive an invitation to a wedding. It's my first formal invitation since the days of confirmations and bar mitzvahs.

"Will you come with me to this wedding?" I ask Jenny.

"Are you inviting me to a wedding?"

"I'd like you to be my guest at this wedding. It says here *and guest*. That'd be you."

"I'd be delighted," Jenny says. "Will you come with me to mine? I got invited to one, too."

"Whose?"

"Somebody's."

"Of course I will come to somebody's wedding," I say. "Maybe you need some normal people responsibilities, you know. Like one job. Just a part-time job somewhere. Waitress again."

"Sounds horrible."

"There's a Help Wanted sign in the pharmacy window."

"Sounds horrible. No."

"You'll learn how many drams go into a dram. You'll be able to steal drugs."

I suggest we get out of the house, even to the diners along the boulevard, but Jenny says let's just get delivery.

I have to force her to leave the house.

She meets me on the steps of the Metropolitan Museum of Art, which is what we always call it.

We pay 50 cents each, using my Ben Franklin half-dollars.

Once inside we head for the emptiest ancient gallery. All of the unknown men. A few unknown women. The gods, they have names. Like the play of torn shadows in a movie from the 30s and we realize everyone doing the acting is long dead. We mimic the globular expressions of sculpted deities and share a laugh. We go upstairs, stand in front of "Mademoiselle V. . . in the Costume of an Espada." We move from gallery to gallery mocking and mimicking and aping the widescreen canvases, the ancient stories retold, filled with so many decisions, and we become angels strumming, elders with walking sticks, or the little remorseful man with the yellowest halo, who needs the king's chiropractor, who can't catch up to the crucifixion because he holds the whole gospel in his cracking spine, more ashamed than everyone else to be a part of art history, far enough behind so that his back is more visible than his front.

I think about Jenny's back on the pitcher's mound, when she wasn't facing me. How much danger I think she's in, when I can't see her face.

A Velázquez has been deaccessed, shit! But the placard is there. It's being restored, it'll only take a moment, and we are the ones who are peeling.

The men are slumping.

We are peeling, slumping, we are missing paintings, beyond restoration, forgeries fit for a king.

○

It's the middle of the night, and Krista Kaplan's texting me. She's stuck in the office overnight on an urgent Omaha need. The prospect is testing the team's responsiveness by imposing an accelerated deadline on the current phase of the sales cycle. They've asked us the most dreaded question in business: tell us what you do.

"Help puppy! Help!" Krista writes. "Spreckman is practicing his golf swing and thinks we'll be here all night! Help me!"

At first I refuse to write back. I'm sick of having my own responsiveness tested. But her messages keep coming, premiere text pulse, an illusion that Krista's texting effort is the effort of Krista the human being.

I have an idea. I'll leave a note, borrow Jenny's car and drive into the city, pick Krista up and take her out to breakfast. By the time I get back to Queens, Jenny will still be asleep. If Krista wants to have sex, we'll have sex, and I'll leave before anything on me has the chance to stick.

I'm coming up, I'm coming up is what I hum to myself as I drive through the dawn into the city and idle on Pine Street, until I'm forced to idle on Broad Street, until I finally get smart and find a spot on William before a cop moves me along and I have to circle the building for what feels like hours. About twenty minutes after that, Krista appears. I get out of the car and open her door. Her natural tan from St. Kitts hasn't faded. Her sun-lightened hair, curly not straightened, nests in her jacket's faux-fur hood. She wears a black hoodie with white drawstring at the neck, dark jeans, her pink-laced sneakers. She exhales a sigh that sounds familiar to me, like she's been honorably discharged from the skyscraper alien army. When I'd been on overnight projects I left in the early morning feeling like her, the only living laborer in New York, until I saw the actual laborers unloading the bread trucks.

"Is this your car?"

"No, my friend's."

"This is your girlfriend's car."

"Yes, but you don't care about that. Remember?"

"That's a little weird."

"I'm letting you in on it, this is my girlfriend's car, you don't care. Remember? You don't care if I let you in on it."

"This is a little weird. You're weird when you're weird, Ty. And it smells like chicken in here. And kind of like puke and kind of like a lot of your cologne."

"An Italian chicken vomited in here. What are the fees on Omaha? How it'd go?"

"Pain, puppy, pain. We work with the most sadistic people. I'm convinced they hate themselves. They were all happy not to go home. Like it was some sleepover. This could've been done by ten, midnight tops, it's not like it really changed from midnight to six. It was supposed to be three slides, a one-pager, then a placemat, then a tri-fold, then we were going to go in with nothing just some bullets on a page. It ended up being like sixty slides. And the value prop still sucks. The value prop is, guess what, we are awesome. Every bullet screams please, whatever you do, don't hire us. Plus no one has any idea what to say at the meeting."

"I can imagine." I drive Big Red uptown, my eyes darting to the sidewalks. The people on the pavement make me more comfortable than the cars on the street.

"When work gets like this I have no balance," Krista continues. "The life is exhausted out of me. I start thinking of the stupidest things at the weirdest times. How deadened is my life? I swear it's the people. I never thought I'd meet people this incredibly lame. My Dad says it's the blind leading people with perfect vision."

"Too many cooks ruin the broth," I agree, about to miss a light. Easing into the stop I watch the yellow as it matches, for yellow's part in a functioning stoplight, the yellows of the morning, and the yellows on sidewalk signs or in the coats of the more fashionable workers.

"Something is happening to me. Instead of truthful statements sounding true, or my lies sounding like lies, everything sounds like the same thing."

"You do say the word 'onerous' a lot. And 'consternation.'"

"I know. Why do I do that? Nothing is true or false. No one can tell when I'm being serious and when I'm faking, when I'm lying and telling the truth. It's not like there are flies buzzing around my head, you know, it's like there are flies *in* my head."

"You'll figure it out." For a moment I'm disgusted to be in Manhattan, with Krista, this far away from Jenny. I want to drop Krista off on the corner and drive back to Queens.

"I'm wired," she says. "And this is only the second time I've been in a car in the city. I mean, not a taxi. I mean, we can go anywhere. There's no meter running."

"Are you hungry?"

"Not at all. I ate Thai food all night."

We keep driving uptown. When we get beyond Fifty-Ninth Street the traffic ends. I find an actual parking spot on a side-street between Lexington and Madison, which feels like a miracle. Then we walk west, toward the park, into a neighborhood of private garages and family pharmacies.

"I never asked you about St. Kitts."

"It's beautiful. This is what I love about the city," Krista says, kissing my street-side cheek, "every few blocks, another city. I miss the city even when I go back to my apartment and I'm technically still here."

I want to say *it's just Seventy-Something Street*, but I don't. And anyway, I agree.

We cross Madison, walk south along Fifth and the park. Krista runs into the street and ducks down behind a car. I walk forward cautiously. She runs out around the car, plants herself and tries to karate kick me. I put myself in a defensive stance, fists up, and make a karate noise.

We hug, kiss, cross the street to the park side and turn into the park at Inventor's Row. We stop before a statue of a man holding what looks like a gas tank. We climb over the benches that line the path, so we can read about the inventor. It's Samuel Morse, the inventor of Morse code, and the tank is his telegraph.

"Sam Morse. One of those guys you don't know, who is so important. How many people you think tap and beep here?"

"We're probably not going to be the first," I say.

"Tap Morse a question."

I tap the foot of the statue.

"What'd you ask?"

"Say a soldier dies during World War I and is cryogenically preserved and brought back to life in the present day. What will he say when he hears there was a World War II? Will he say, 'I died in vain?'"

"Poor Morse," Krista says. "Pigeon shit isn't his only problem." She taps.

"What'd you tap?"

"I want a croissant. The furthest thing from Thai food. Sorry. I just got really, really tired."

We start walking back to the car, saying nothing.

"Let's drive back to your place."

"There's no parking there."

"Well, let's take a cab."

"I need to tell you something, Ty. I met someone over vacation. In St. Kitts. Danny. I think you and I need to stop doing this."

"I have no clue what we're doing."

"I've been honest with you about us and we need to end it here."

Fuming, I picture Danny, having his way with the creamsicle bathing suit, having his way with the white suit. I picture Krista and Danny snorkeling with sea turtles, bottoms of tanned feet touching nothing but white sand.

"End what?" I say. "You haven't been honest. You said to be yourself, just let me in on it."

"Well, I'm letting you in on it. I didn't think it was going to get like it is so quickly."

"With me, or Danny?"

My phone rings. I see messages from Jenny. She's up. She's feeling pretty good. She's asking if I drove Big Red to the diner to pick us up some breakfast. She's not sure if she wants bacon egg and cheese on a roll, or sausage egg and cheese on a bagel.

"I have to get the car back to Queens."

"It's okay I'll get a cab," Krista says.

"No. No. I'll drive you. It's crazy, you know, that your Dad takes you to islands. He takes you to the island of St. Kitts. He pays for you to live on the island of Manhattan…"

"You don't know anything about me."

"You've never had to work for anything in your life. Yet you're so good at working. Funny how that happens."

"Whatever, I'll see you tomorrow."

"You know, my Dad's never been to an island. Except for Manhattan."

"Okay, so what?"

"Sometimes I think my Dad might be happier if he just gave up."

"What do you mean?"

"I just want to know the exact minute he's going to die, you know, so I can prepare for it. Don't you want to know."

"That's foul," Krista says. "Don't you know the power of words? That something like that could come true just from you saying it?"

Instead of saying that words don't make people die, I agree and say I don't know their power.

We're standing in front of Jenny's car.

It feels hot with Krista's anger.

"I really wanted to build something with you," I say. "Pre-Danny, of course."

"You can't be pissed off and tell me you love me, Ty. It doesn't work like that."

"Does Danny know where you are right now? We've been kissing all morning. You're such a bitch."

"Give me your girlfriend's keys," Krista says.

"Great. You can drive."

She holds the keys up, as if to present their power, and runs them along the driver-side of the hood, making a jittery line of white scratch against the car's paint. She throws the keys at my feet.

I bend down to pick them up, slotting one key through two of my fingers, ready to stand up and punch her in the face.

"This is my girlfriend's car," I say. "You know? It's not mine."

"I know. Because for as weird as you are, I didn't think you'd have a *My Little Pony* keychain."

I look down at the keys and notice, for the first time, a rainbow pony grinning back at me.

"You make me nervous," Krista says. "You and your girlfriend need to grow up." Krista walks away, to the corner of Madison.

I watch her put her hand up to hail a cab.

She has to wait a few seconds, since all the cabs at this time in the morning are on their way downtown. I get in the car and drive back to Queens, upset yet relieved.

When Jenny notices the hood scratch a few days later, she can't remember if she parked Big Red somewhere where someone would do something like that.

"Have we been to Brooklyn lately?" she asks.

"I don't think so. It's a mystery to me, too," I say.

And for a very long time I make fun of her for still using a *My Little Pony* keychain.

○

Krista and I both interview for the same regional role. She gets the promotion and goes on the road a lot.

She texts me from Hartford: *I'm in the capital of Connecticut*, but she doesn't call me *puppy* anymore. Now I'm just a dog like everyone else.

Tweed tells me he's happy to have her out of the office, so her breasts won't be flying all over the place. He takes that back, if it offends me. I tell him it doesn't. He tells me he thinks they were making it hard for me to concentrate.

I never see Krista anymore, but one Saturday morning we do run into each other on the Metro Level of Bloomingdales. I am handling some of the dearer fabrics. When I feel a fabric, I feel a man, until I spot Krista's manicured nose near hip-hop golf wear. I am still touching the sweater, but now all I feel is her.

If we saw each other on Third Avenue instead of the Metro Level, we might have kept on walking. Under the retail lights, though, we must face each other.

"You're out early," I say, only now smelling my own stink.

"I buy a lot of clothes down here."

It's spring, and she wears what I guess to be a men's store black sweater. Her slender throat gives the ribbed collar life, like a cotton necklace. Her hair is dark and curly, her lips bare yet pink. My blues, whatever hue, they deepen.

"I don't know what you're on, but this week sucked."

"Oh yeah," I respond. "Next week is going to suck, too."

"I'm excited to finally be home on a Saturday, though. My new plan, when I'm home, is to not go out Friday night so my Saturdays are normal, and from there it's just one step to not go out Saturday night, so my Sundays are normal. Anyway, I'm going to walk down to the village after this."

"I could join you on your walk. I feel pretty normal today."

"Thanks, but I want to be by myself," she says, making a gesture of exclusion with her hand, and that's when I notice she's wearing an engagement ring.

"We never got an email about that," I say, motioning toward the ring. "Congratulations."

"Thanks."

"Danny's a lucky man."

"I've been meaning to tell you. I want to do something about the car."

"It was my fault."

"Not really. I want to do something. You just made me so nervous."

"So you do think it was my fault."

"No. No I don't. I want to do something. I'm in the office all day next Friday. Calendar a lunch for us. My treat."

"I might have to get lobster on my pizza."

She smiles, walks toward men's formalwear. I watch her go. She takes all of it with her. She has in overabundance, like her beauty, the nerve to walk away.

○

It's time to clean up. It's time to get better and get ahead on getting ahead. I throw out my coke, weed, tea, coffee, cigarettes. I make an appointment with Doc Jason, who comes highly recommended to write easy scripts for Adderall, Xanax, Ativan, Klonopin, Viagra, Cialis, Vicodin and Lunesta.

I schedule my visit for lunchtime, still take an hour's lunch, and then head to Doc Jason's lair. The office is in a no-man's-land stretch of Madison in the 30s, but the waiting room is Brooklyn hip. There are granola bars, flavored lip balms, a basket overflowing with Skittles-rainbow LifeStyles (a handwritten invitation to *shroud the rainbow* taped to the edge of the basket) and tri-fold marketing materials crammed with useful tips.

Do you have ADHD?

Are you at risk for coronary heart disease?

Now, Discover Your Strengths.

I sit below an *Ascenseur pour l'échafaud* poster and choose a men's magazine from the cascade of periodicals. The husky front-page model wears a long coat the color of Christmas, his five o'clock shadow in mountain time zone. I consume bullet-points on what a man needs to be:

- A man needs to visit his doctor on a regular basis;
- A man needs to dress up a t-shirt with a blazer;
- A pocket square gives the most casual outfit a supreme touch of class; and
- Don't just rub and rinse: soap should sit on the skin for a few minutes to reach its full potential.

These are all practical ideas I'll forget when I put the magazine down. A shoegaze version of "Be My Baby" pipes through the office speakers. Big, big guitars. I tap the beat with my weak foot, heel on the first three notes, toes on the last. It isn't as difficult as I want it to be, not as difficult as brushing my teeth with the other hand to ward off Alzheimer's, which I then remember I keep forgetting to do.

Finally, my name is called. A petite, pierced, purple-haired nurse escorts me to a moodily-lit examination room. She requests that I remove my clothes and enter arms in a paper gown.

"That's not really why I'm here," I say, fingering my tie.

She asks again in the same voice. She leaves the room. I change. It takes her a lifetime to return. She records my vital signs.

"Your blood pressure is very high."

"Is that good?"

"Your temperature is 104."

"Is that high?"

"What can we do for you today?"

"I have some questions for Doc Jason."

"What questions?"

"How does it go? I mean, what do I tell you and what do I tell the doctor?"

"We just like to get an idea of why you're here."

"My ear hurts," I say, scratching the skin on the side of my nose. "Will my insurance fully cover this visit?"

"I don't know. Why are you visiting?"

Doc Jason knocks and walks in at the same time. He's tall and wears thick, red-rimmed eyeglasses. He isn't wearing a tie, or even a lab coat. He smells clean. His hair is blue.

The nurse says "ear," like she's heard about my ear before, hands Doc Jason my file and excuses herself from the examination room.

"So which ear should I talk into," Doc Jason winds up, "so we can figure out what's wrong with the other one!"

"Haha."

"Wait a second, did I really just say that?"

"You did. I didn't expect you to, but you did. I'm kind of glad you did. I need my primary care physician to make jokes like that."

"Who *am* I?" Doc Jason wonders.

"There's not a lot wrong with my ear, really. Sometimes it hurts, I guess. Wait, it actually hurts right now."

"That's strange."

"I mean it's probably because I'm talking about it, right? The power of suggestion."

"That's very possible, and probably true."

"I know. I'm just looking for some pharmacological balance and I heard you can help me with that. I can't get hard sometimes. Not really, really hard. I used to be with this girl who got me hard like that, but that's over. Now I need drugs to replace her. I have problems relaxing on long flights. I can't concentrate when I have deadlines. It's difficult to fall asleep at home, too, because I live with my father and a death metal guitarist. I work out a lot and sometimes have really sore muscle pains, and I don't want to take more than four Advil."

Doc Jason turns his Risperdal-labeled pen. "Do you have a history of heart problems?"

"Not your kind."

"There are always four people in the room when two people are having sex. Did I just say that?"

"You did. Who said that? That's good."

"Not sure. Nixon? Yogi Berra?"

"That makes sense. Me, her, Dick Cheney, the barista."

"Do you understand how all of these drugs work? I'll print you out the materials."

"That's wonderful."

"Viagra, por example, will solve your physical problem, but it won't arouse you. That's still on you."

"What's arousal? I mean, I can get around that. Can you test me for AIDS and everything else, too?"

"Are you a homosexual?"

"No. Not really."

"Do you have sex with men?"

"Never, no."

Jason's mood shifts. He taps his Risperdal-labeled pen against his Leuchtturm 1917. He pushes up his glasses and I notice how long he holds the frame. I think to myself that every time he re-raises his glasses, he recalls a childhood of being tortured for wearing them. "Do you see any mental health doctors? Ever been to therapy?"

"I mean, I know you're a real doctor, you don't want to see me, you didn't go to medical school for this. I know doctors say they don't allow pharma reps into their offices but it's not like that matters, like you're a restaurant that only serves free-range chicken, or those antebellum organic cotton petticoats darned by free-range slaves. You know that cartoon?"

He looks down at my empty file, says, "What's on your mind, Tyrone?"

"Well, I've never been to therapy. I mean, my family is not a therapy family. Even when my Mom died, no one else talked to anyone. Why let it out when you can keep it all inside? Basically I'm just wondering, if you come from a happy family, which I do, can you ever go too far?"

"They'll usually be a limit, right, something inside you, like remembering you were protected, to keep that from happening."

"Yeah. I remember being protected. But I want to touch that limit, and show it how much I care."

"Americans, you know, live in a psychological slum."

"Wow, isn't that true."

"It is, isn't it? Who said that?"

"I don't know. It's good."

"Isn't it?"

I thank Doc Jason and assure him I'll follow-up. I even agree to keep a small diary where I will jot down my usual and unusual feelings after dosing myself with his amphetamine salts.

At the front desk, I'm told my co-pay is all there is for today. I grab some granola bars, lip balms, a dozen condoms. I fold the prescriptions, put them in the inner pocket of my bag. I ride the elevator down to the street and I suddenly find myself facing the paneling and weeping.

I heave and chant "world, world, world."

Congested, it comes out "whirl, whirl, whirl."

○

I call Jenny because I want to see what the Viagra does. She's loft-sitting in Chinatown for an editor she met at one of her Brooklyn parties. The common area of the loft, cluttered with mismatched furniture, resembles the as-is section of an IKEA. Carryon and checked baggage blocks the standard TV. The tenants seem to be both present and absent at the same time, posing for a reality camera that isn't rolling. None of the housemates talk or even regard the other person while standing right next to them and performing intimate household activities.

"This is a psychological slum," I say to Jenny.

"Everyone knows that," she says. "That makes it a mansion."

In the communal kitchen we drink Portuguese wine labeled with the editor's name, Anne. We use the communal sushi-making set to roll cucumber-avocado maki. Every piece crumbles. The cucumbers are too big. One of the drawers in the kitchen has hundreds of reduced-sodium soy sauce packets. We open dozens of them and push the threadbare maki through dark puddles of liquid salt.

"I bet you Anne has sexy undies," Jenny says. "Do you want me to put some on?"

"I don't think you're going to have to do anything."

"You're taking a sexy pill, I should slide sexy undies on."

"Stop it."

Jenny sings, "Put Anne's sexy undies on, doo-da, doo-da. Put Anne's sexy undies on, doo, da doo da day!"

She sits on top of me, holds her breasts from underneath. She leans down to Anne's table, rubs her hands together to warm Anne's warming lube.

"You're as hard as you always are."

"No, it's more," I say, and it hurts. The loss of sensation, the whole reason for sex, goes unlisted as a side effect of Viagra.

For all the things my penis enters, nothing is tighter than the history of medicine. And now that I know I can stay hard forever, it's time to get married.

○

Everyone seems to be getting married. On my way to weddings I read dope *Atlantic Monthly* articles about how nobody is.

Jenny and I fall in love with attending weddings.

"When's the next one?" she asks.

"Please be my plus-one," I say.

"I would love to attend with you."

She wears the same black dress and I wear the same Chinese suit and Italian tie. The brides are so beautiful. There are two kinds of wedding dresses, princess and not. Men aren't sure what their brides will be until they're revealed and by then it's too late. Couples stand on makeshift altars, shedding nuptial jitters, the unusual combination of unease and boredom, their wide constant smiles earning them the prize of sexual redemption. Whoever they

hurt before, whoever they abandoned yesterday, now, in the name
of God and the State of New York, it's all good. Sometimes, God
doesn't show up. Amateur service leaders make jokes about the
power vested in them by the internet. I want to drown them as the
swan melts.

Usually I'm Jenny's plus one, but there's one where she's mine.
An Israeli accountant weds a Persian chemical engineer. I met this
accountant in a summer school gym class, where we bonded over
what losers we were for failing gym. I still hear her asking, "what's
the girl version of the squat thrust, and will I still pass if I can't do
it?" She talked about leaving Queens and moving to Manhattan but
this Persian engineer she's marrying lives far out enough in Queens
that I know this girl, when she gets back from her honeymoon in
Puerto Vallarta, will get lost in Queens forever.

Jenny and I sit at table 12 with people we don't know. We
discuss the difference between Iranians and Persians. There are
many things I don't know about Iran. There are nearly 80 million
people in the country. It snows there. One thing I know for certain,
after gaining all of this knowledge, is that I never want to attend an
Israeli-Persian wedding ever again. It just has so many official
combinations—son dancing with mother, daughter dancing with
father, nephew dancing with niece, cousin dancing with uncle—
that I deviously imagine the event programmed by the Marquis de
Sade, after being sentenced to a lifetime of wedding planner prison
for his role in the celebration of sodomy. There's this passage from
the *120 Days* I think about sometimes to arouse myself. A criminal
discovers the most pleasurable thing he can imagine is to turn out
a young girl's ass while, outside a Magritte window only de Sade
could have prophesized, the girl watches her father being lynched.
Might this be the greatest orgasm ever recorded, the one that

criminal had? A primal scream. And that poor girl, she was lucky, she knew exactly when her father would die.

That's how bored I am at this wedding. And I discover I've already slept with not only the bride but all of her bridesmaids and much of the groom's immediate family, too, except for the groom's sister, whom I worry about as she totters past me in her tight carnation-colored dress, more the condensed milk than the flower. When she looks at me and her eyes say—*take me, I'm the only one left*—I realize that I am, more than anything else I may be, a fucker of brides. And it's not like this gets me a speech. *Now we'd like to bring up a young man who knew Esther a very long time ago. Esther and this man both failed gym. In college. Esther and this man did sit-ups together.* No, that never happens. Esther only knows one man now, and he's the man he best remembers. The way his baby tells the story, well, that's what the story is.

You don't catch a bride's name at a wedding, even though it's written everywhere. Christina Goldberg, Tiffany Solowitz, Susie Greenberg.

I'm invited to Krista Kaplan's wedding, and I also chip in for the office gift. *So Beautiful* is the name I give to each bride. It's so often how brides are addressed and defined, by friends and family passing right by them. *So Beautifuls* are dark, sharp, toned, young, head-on into careers, with defined triceps, well-socialized. *So Beautiful*'s diamond-laid hair piece, her pastel heels placed casually atop a pale blue hope chest. She has no time to think. How lucky to be a bride with no time for reflection. All of the things she must do to get ready. All of the women hounding her. A private moment scheduled. Her mother driving her nuts. She is touched, touched-up, pressed to be scrolled by on feeds.

You've got to look good for the big day.

Those weeks when I know they'll be a weekend wedding, I take it easy on calorie consumption. Medium-sized bananas and apples, no fries. I sit at table 12 or its buffet-style equivalent. I bring along sedatives, maybe a joint, not that I need anything to aid my munchies because love makes me hungry and there's nothing I won't swallow come wedding time. After they are defined as man and wife and the celebrants file out into the cocktail area, I rush ahead so I can gulp down my first palmfuls of nuts from the snifters atop the open bars. Oriental mix, candied walnut mix, honey-roasted clusters, sesame sticks and wasabi peas. At cocktail hour I scout the waiters and their trays of spring rolls and quarter-sized pizza bites costing Dad $7.50 a pop. I dip those pies in chili sauce, drown them in chili sauce, drown the caramelized onion mini-toasts in the cocktail sauce that comes with the mini-skewers of Gulf shrimp, the skewers of non-Gulf shrimp, the regular French fries, seasoned French fries, sweet potato French fries and turkey-burger sliders which I dip in stoneground mustard, ranch, ketchup and round back again to the chili sauce. Satiated, stuffed, unable to swallow anything else, I'm just getting started. I swallow *So Beautiful*'s white almonds, her cocktail-hour Anthony Braxton jazz selection, Cajun truffle fries dipped in Creole mustard, Dijon ranch, Sriracha veggie spring roll chili sauce and I prepare myself for the main course sides, *haricots verts* in buttery shallot reductions, strange mushrooms, curried cashews courtesy of Bethany Katz and Cordelia Edelstein, so sad her nana Bunny Edelstein couldn't be with us today. I chew fresh green leaves, seasonal leaves, tri-colored leaves, wild perennial garden leaves in a lite balsamic vinaigrette, many of the green leaves of Jenny's salad (she doesn't like plum tomatoes, so I get those too, because no beefsteak tomato has ever been served at any wedding we've attended) and I never say no to more pink sea salt, more freshly cracked black pepper, more fresh parmesan over my fourteen tubes of handmade pasta. I swallow one of Jenny's friend's salads since she can't digest foliage in a tight dress. I break apart and lovingly dip everyone's dinner rolls in my oily bubbles of warm vinaigrette or spicy veggie chili sauce, but the flatbreads slathered in butter I garnish with dried cranberries.

Wives yell at their texting husbands: stop texting, will you please stop texting, stop texting, who *are* you texting, anyway? Everyone you know is here. I've got nothing to say. There's no salmon I won't finish. My salmon, Jenny's salmon, her camp friend's salmon, her ex-ex-boyfriend's salmon, an aunt's salmon, a mysterious piece of salmon, traditional *patatas bravas* dipped in salmon juice, ketchup, mustard, and peanut-Thai veggie spring roll sauce.

During the speeches I run out of patience and I run out of food. Speeches lovingly and tearfully delivered by mothers and fathers or stepmothers and stepfathers who—and really, it's been said so many times this weekend already but it can't be said enough—have been with the family since the birth of divorce, and who are more like blood than some of the true blood who yawn and seethe during their speeches. Speeches by close friends of the family, Bunnies who held on to make it to this day, current cancers, cancers that won, cancers that are winning, cancers that can still be beat. Unable to upwell with emotion any longer I excuse myself from table 12. I pretend my vibrating phone is ringing with an urgent business call, point to it with a grimace as if to say, Money Never Sleeps. I walk out of the hall and into the city, stand out in the night lights of the Avenue of the Americas or Times Square Broadway. I take a few puffs of my joint as the tourists from the American interior stroll by, swinging their Disney bags, starving for heroes. I return to the lobby to use the bathroom. I urinate, wash my hands thoroughly from the faucet the attendant turns on for me and I accept his proffered cloth napkin to dry my hands and then deposit the napkin in his waist-high wicker basket. I am comforted by the idea I haven't wasted paper, but I will waste water when this barely used cloth napkin is washed. I use some lotion, maybe St. Ives, maybe Neutrogena. I'm stoned, so maybe that's why I think the attendant resembles Michael Mann's dad, because he's the first black man I've spoken to since Michael's wake, the father of my featherbrained friend, who asked me to sign Michael's memory book, who, like me, couldn't reach the toilet bowl when he pissed.

The attendant, who I now realize isn't Michael Mann's dad, says my dress shoes are sharp. He is a human being. He is standing in front of me. I ask him an innocent question, the Giants, the Knicks, maybe the Rangers, we start a conversation. Almost immediately I have no idea what this man is saying, so I say yeah, yeah, yeah, yeah, eyeing the golden cinnamons on his sink ledge, the Skin Bracer, the D&G Cool Blue and the Drakkar, wondering which scent I might want to take back with me to table 12, to neutralize the scents I've introduced onto my person since excusing myself from the table. I see mouthwash on the sink counter. I realize that the attendant's way of talking is a lot like what I sound like when I'm gargling mouthwash. He speaks, I answer yeah, yeah, yeah, yeah, and I ask him for mouthwash to do some gargling myself. Then I ask him for a Newport 100, put it in my suit jacket's inner pocket. I don't really care if he thinks Bonds deserves the Hall of Fame. It makes no difference to me if he thinks Spike should cool it on the sidelines at the Garden. I drop three or four single dollar bills into his tip jar, another kind of wicker basket, on the ledge next to combs soaking in Barbicide. White Devil is nothing if not an accurate tipper, so in order to redeem myself for not paying attention to anything this man said, I overtip. At weddings, surrounded by so many celebrants going for broke, money seems to have a negative value, or no value at all. At least to me, if not to this man who dug my sharp shoes, the man I choose not to suffer.

○

I go all by myself to Krista's wedding. Mr. Fucker of Brides plus Nobody. I hang with other co-workers and we all do some dry-heave networking after our thirty-fifth Heinekens. And what the hell am I doing here, what delusion brought me to this yeasty catering hall? How is it possible for me to attend Krista's wedding with raw memories of a broken heart? It shows me nothing but the monster in my own. I exercise it very well. The monster grows stronger the more I repeat the same actions. Who is pain for, some version of me that takes it, a version of me I'd like to think is an enduring self? But I am not an enduring self. That version of me only exists when I place myself in situations which promise to bring me pain. Situations I think I belong in. If I just let myself be happy, this enduring self gets up and walks away. So much for routines.

During the dancing, Krista approaches me in her simple gown, her veil like mosquito netting and I'm the mosquito. She steals me away from one of her buzzing bridesmaids in order to tell me she doesn't think I'm weird, she's really sorry for what happened, and she still has opinions on my romantic possibilities, and also to warn me to cease engaging her bridesmaid, whom she thinks pesty and obscene, a stand-up compromise from Danny's side of the family. She swears to me—even at this event, her wedding to another man, she still goes on praising her version of my romantic life—that I am not the epic lover I often pretend to be, a lover of many women, but I am the lyrical lover of my girlfriend with the *My Little Pony* keychain. The great, careful lover of one other soul. Any soul, that is, other than Krista's.

"That's cool," I say. "Where are you going on your honeymoon?"

"Rome. You look happy."

"That's funny."

"What's funny, Rome?"

"No, the word happy."

"You're one of the happiest people I know, Ty. Even though you're always acting miserable around me."

"That's funny. Rome. I should go there. Or I should go to St. Kitts and throw myself in Mt. Misery."

"Go to Rome instead."

"I'll go to Rome," I say. "After you leave."

O

It's time for another wedding. Jenny and I dance all night. Do the bookends on cue. We dance "Signed, Sealed, Delivered" and point to each other on the yours. We dance to new hits. We dance "You're The First, The Last, My Everything." We admit our love is still doomed, our relationship still broken, we lie together on the bed in pieces, waiting for the sacred light, broken apart and not even bothering to snap ourselves back together. When we desire, all we desire is one drag, long arms to strangle the guilt. We need more from our relationships, and in our understanding of relationships, more includes all of this.

"I'm really going to miss you, Ty."

"I'm right here."

"You're the only one who knows where to go next. You always know where we can go next."

"I know where we can go next. There's a new bar over on Sixth, it's like a block from here. Or there's that one in the 20s between Second and Third that we love."

"That you love."

"There's so many places we could go next. We could go to a bar. We could crash the afterparty at the Marriott Marquis. We could walk between the skyscrapers. We could walk down by the river."

"How am I going to know where to go next without you?" Jenny asks.

A gentleman, I remember, is someone who can play the accordion, but doesn't.

"I'm right here," I say. "Without you, how will I ever know the band is coming back out? I count on you for endings. You know the boys are reprising the riff."

Coffee and a selection of herbal teas. Blueberries, raspberries, blackberries, strawberries, red grapes, currants, green grapes, artisanal Butterfingers. Sparkling grapefruit slices. Nonpareils sprinkled like rose petals over a marriage bed, gingersnaps, Swedish Fish, Norwegian Bears, Finlandia peppermints. Wow, look at the cake. Tubs and also tubes of M&Ms and M&M bark, torpedoes loaded with licorice nibs and twists. Megaton bombs of double-dipped toffee caramels, chocolate cherries, cashew orphans, cannons of peanut brittle and pecan patties. Doggie bags. Take your treats home. Never forget us. Doggie bags for treats announcing the new couple's names, the June dateline with euro-periods separating month year and day.

Before packing up for the evening I turn to Jenny and tell her some of my observations, my smart and funny observations, how this wedding seems different from all the other weddings because tonight the sorbet had a powerful minty taste. That intermezzo was a real palate cleanser. And Jenny yawns. Inspiration floods her mouth. She yawns more and more whenever I speak. And each time they are deeper, sleepier yawns.

"Remember that time I told you not to meet another me, because that me would just be me and it'd suck for me?"

"Yeah."

"Well," Jenny says, yawning, "I think I'm another me now."

"Look at that."

"And the new me doesn't want you anymore."

I need to turn her yawning into something positive, the way a parent smells its baby's shit as sweet.

"Go to hell, Ty," Jenny yawns. "Hell, now."

When Jenny yawns, and that's a good deal of what I see her do these days, it doesn't mean she's sleepy. And it doesn't mean I'm making her bored. But it also doesn't mean more believable excuses, like it's hot in this room, it's been such a late night and maybe yawning is her allergic reaction to decaf coffee, the way NyQuil jacks her up.

She's yawning because that's just how she is, I know that, she yawns.

No, none of that is what yawning means. Maybe, as it is said, yawning is a silent scream for coffee. Or maybe, like Kerouac thought, a kitty yawns because she realizes there's nothing to do. Maybe yawning means you are so very interesting to me I cannot bear to concentrate on what you say. Yawning means I love you oh so very much because around you I feel safe. And then I yawn. Not from boredom, rehearsed love or sleepy nearness, instead a fear of cold causes my yawn, cold stated as a question: If I am forced to, how will I ever face the world with wakefulness, with open eyes and a closed mouth, when this woman is no longer yawning at me everywhere I speak?

That question charms me with its Jennytude. There is little left to do at the end of the night but yawn and yawn again.

Acknowledgments

Jenny in Corona benefited from readings by Patrick Jehle, David Ewald, Carolyn Tate, Andy Mozina, Brenna Kischuk and Rebecca Makkai. Thanks to Summer Literary Seminars, The Ragdale Foundation, The Chicago Public Library, and Kopi Café, where major parts of this book were (re)written. Thanks to my wife, Betsy Ross, who read this manuscript more times than a spouse should have to. Thanks to my parents. Thanks to the supportive writing community in Chicago.

The following pieces of writing are referenced in *Jenny in Corona*:

Another Country by James Baldwin
Anton Von Webern by Hans and Rosaleen Moldenhauer
Drawings by Lee Lozano
Give My Regards to Eighth Street by Morton Feldman
Illness as Metaphor by Susan Sontag
Open City by Teju Cole
The 120 Days of Sodom by Marquis de Sade
The Metamorphosis by Franz Kafka
The Farewell Symphony by Edmund White
"And The Days Are Not Full Enough" by Ezra Pound
"A Woman Waits for Me" by Walt Whitman
"November Graveyard" by Sylvia Plath
"Prayer for my Mother" by Pier Paolo Pasolini
"The Emperor of Ice-Cream" and "The Snowman" by Wallace Stevens

"Waiting" by William Carlos Williams
"Whore" by Mayhem

About the Author

Stuart Michael Ross came via caesarian April 17, 1977, 10:54 A.M at Brooklyn Hospital. *Jenny in Corona* is his first novel.

About Tortoise Books

Slow and steady wins in the end, even in publishing. Tortoise Books is dedicated to finding and promoting quality authors who haven't yet found a niche in the marketplace—writers producing memorable and engaging works that will stand the test of time.

Learn more at www.tortoisebooks.com, find us on Facebook, or follow us on Twitter @TortoiseBooks